DAYLIGHT

Russell James had seven years of military education before opting out to see the world. Among many jobs held down in a wandering career, his favourites include the dawn shift on a Mediterranean radio station and backstage work at the Old Vic. He has founded his own business consultancy, and handles special projects in consumer and charity marketing.

Russell James is married, with two children, and lives in Gloucestershire. Gollancz have published all three of his thrillers, *Underground*, *Daylight* and *Payback*.

Also by Russell James in Gollancz Crime

UNDERGROUND

DAYLIGHT

by

Russell James

GOLLANCZ CRIME

Gollancz Crime is an imprint of Victor Gollancz Ltd
14 Henrietta Street, London WC2E 8QJ

First published in Great Britain 1990
by Victor Gollancz Ltd

First Gollancz Crime edition 1991

A catalogue record for this book
is available from the British Library

ISBN 0-575-05092-6

Printed and bound in Great Britain
by Cox & Wyman Ltd, Reading

For Jill, Kate and Sarah,
who were there all the time.

With thanks to Stella and Georgia.

It happened in London and Leningrad in the peaceful summer of 1989—a few short months before Communism collapsed in Europe. I should have seen the signs. I should have known my task would be harder than it looked. I should have known that people could get killed.

LONDON

I

The guy driving the car is called Louis. He was in Pentonville with me. He was serving three years for aggravated burglary, and didn't get parole. So we had two years together.

I didn't get parole either. Sentences of five years or over usually don't. Especially if the offence involves drugs or violence.

When they added my sentences together, there was a total of eight years. Prisoners get a third off anyway, whatever we do, so that gave me five years four months, before parole. With parole, I could have come out in under three years. But I didn't. I could have come out in under four. But I didn't.

The third year that I was knocked back, I saw it coming. That second time I had let myself hope: refusal hurt. So the third time I didn't bother. When they gave me the sheet of paper to write my side, my "Representations", I wrote "Same as last year", and left it at that. When the committee member came to interview me, I talked about football. I said we both knew I wouldn't get it, so why pretend? We just chatted. There was no reason to play along. Everyone knows the rules: more than five years—little chance—a few months maybe; eight years plus violence—not a hope of parole.

Eight years was stiff, I thought. The judge said he wanted to make an example. He and I—we had the same motive: to deter. He wanted to stop young criminals sticking a gun in their pocket and going out to bust a place apart. I wanted to stop old criminals busting *my* place apart.

The gun never came out of my pocket.

Anyway, judge, I learned my lesson: no guns—not any more. If I hadn't carried it, my sentence would have been half. I'd have got parole. And I wouldn't be here now.

When I stepped outside that big prison gate last January, I thought I'd learned those lessons. There I was, twenty-six years old, out on the pavement for the first time in over five years, and what had I got? An old-fashioned suit with forty quid in the pocket. And waiting at home, a dying mother.

I've changed my suit now.

Louis parks the car just along from the front door. He has his jacket collar up. It may be high summer, but it is seven in the morning and it is not warm. The whole street is in shadow. These are tall houses. The sun won't be over the roofs for a couple of hours.

I leave Louis in the car, pick up my bag, and approach the front door. It is not locked. It never is. I climb the two flights of stairs to the girl's flat, put my bag on the floor and unzip it. I bring out the heavy chain-cutter, then stand up and ring the bell. Nothing happens. I ring again.

Inside the flat, someone is moving. I hear a scuffling behind the door.

"Who is it?" comes a girl's voice.

"Postman. Signature, please."

She mumbles something, and I imagine her tying her dressing-gown cord. She opens the door six inches. It is on a chain, as I thought it would be. Through the crack, her face appears. She is as black as midnight and built for late hours. I put my foot in the gap and raise my cutters to the chain.

"Gonna let me in?" I ask, as I snip through the links.

She is a light little thing and causes no trouble. I slip straight across her sitting-room into the bedroom. Calvin starts sitting up in bed.

I lean against the doorpost and say "Hi, Cal."

He peers over the foot of the bed to see what it is hangs heavy in my hand. "Thought you carrying a Colt 45," he says. He speaks like a Trinidadian, but he's been here all his life.

"I ain't looking for trouble," I say. "But we gotta go now."

"Where to?"

He knows the answer. His eyes are blurred with sleep. His black face has gone pale as tea.

The girl is grabbing at me from behind, so I reach round and pull her into the room. I tell Calvin to explain.

He tries to shush her, but it only wakes her voice. She starts

12

yelling out, asking what's happening. When she closes in on me to hammer on my chest. I lift her bodily and take her kicking to the bed.

"Shut her up, Cal," I say. "We don't want the neighbours in."

Calvin leans forward in bed, and fits his hand gently across her mouth. I tell her that no one's gonna hurt her, but she has to stop that shouting. She lies looking up at Calvin. He nods. She stops wriggling.

I tell Calvin to get dressed.

He tries to talk me out of it. He hasn't got the money. He can't get it. Six hundred quid does not come easily.

"Seven hundred," I tell him.

"Seven?"

"There's interest. Gottfleisch says it's seven now."

It's the third time I've called for it. I don't normally do debt-collection, but Gottfleisch says I have to do something. I can't just sit around waiting for the big trip. I have to earn. And I know Calvin. He used to be a friend. It would be easy for me.

"What he going to do to me, Mickey?"

I shrug. I don't want to think about it. I'm just the pick-up man. So the girl starts calling the turn on me: "You taking this man to have him killed. They cut off his hand. What he done to they, anyway? Seven hundred pound! You a butcher. You shit on the ground."

She's got the kind of face that's worth watching even when it's spitting. But I don't like what she's saying. The beef is true.

"It was a accident, man," Calvin says reproachfully. "I on duty at the time. What he want—I hang around let them all get caught?"

I know what he means. Calvin was the driver. Two other so-called professionals were inside removing decorations while he waited in the street. The idiots got in there OK. They took their time on the windows. They traced back the wiring, worked out whether it was the old open circuit or closed, or a newer combination-looped, then made the right kind of short. You know the way that's done? For open-circuit you just snip the wires. For closed, you clip on the jump before you snip. For combination you

13

snip one and jump the other. The trick is, of course, to know which kind you're dealing with. You need a compass. You lay the compass by the wire and watch to see if it twitches. Yes—you need a bypass. No—just snip.

These guys will have known all that. They were not *complete* idiots.

Having fixed the alarm-wire, they cut the glass from the four window-panels, then cut out the cross-piece to make a hole big enough to climb through. This way they need not move the frame itself and set off a recessed contact alarm. All this they did properly. Then they crawled in, cased out the room, and disabled the indoor infra-red. Everything went to plan.

But when they hauled the pictures out the window they got careless. I don't know what they did—stepped on a pressure-pad maybe—but whatever it was, they set off an alarm.

Out they came sharpish, running paintings across the lawn. Back they went for the rest. You always have a few minutes after the alarm begins to ring. Those minutes ticked away. They fetched another pair of pictures. In the front of the car, Calvin was having an abortion. Then they heard the sirens wailing. Calvin roared them out of there at the speed of light. Like he says, he was doing his duty. But he went too fast. He was too eager. He whisked them out of the blue trouble, but wrapped the getaway car round a lamp-post.

Moments of panic. Three men shouting. But the car could still motor, and he limped them all home thinking it a job well done. Gottfleisch did not think so. He billed the damage to the car.

So I do see that Calvin has a point. He is not being treated fairly. But Gottfleisch is the boss here, and bosses are not noted for fair behaviour. Otherwise they would not be bosses.

I'm just the errand boy.

As he gets dressed, his girl is crying. I bring the shutters down. I make like this is some play I'm acting in. It ain't real. I tell Calvin there's no point making a run because he doesn't think I came alone? I suggest maybe Gottfleisch will go easy on him. Maybe he just wanted to scare him a little. Cal tries to believe me.

But apart from Louis, I did come alone. And Louis couldn't stop a tap dripping. You see, the job only pays enough for two of us. We get twenty per cent—a hundred and twenty quid. Between us. This is the kind of money I get up early for. Sixty quid.

From what I've seen of Gottfleisch, he'll add it to Calvin's bill.

Before we leave the room, I allow Calvin another minute with the girlfriend. She is leaking like a cracked teapot. He sits on the bed with his arm around her, trying to console her. You'd think *she* was the one for the car-ride.

When we cruise off in the car, nobody says anything. Louis drives like he's not used to the district. I stare out the window. Cal doesn't want to talk any more. He knows what is coming and so do we. Roughly. I assume he is staring at his hands.

But he ain't.

When I turn to take a peek at him, I find he is concentrating his attention on me. He is staring into the side of my face like he ain't never met me before. Like he's making sure he'll remember me: the guy who betrayed him.

2

So what do you think—that I'm proud about this? That I enjoy it? You think I don't know this is lower than I should ever have stooped, and that I have to get out?

It ain't easy. The truth never is easy. Nor is getting out. Gottfleisch has me trapped. I was lured in with the promise of one big job, and I took some small ones to fill in time. I tried to refuse them. The way I look at it is this: all jobs carry risk, small ones as much as big. Four little jobs carry four times the risk of one big job. I am here for that big one. Let me do that, and I'll slip away content.

It'll put me back on my feet.

I know what you're saying. Here's a guy sentenced to eight years' bird. He comes out twenty-six years old, and what has he learnt? Nothing. Straight back on the dodge.

But what do *you* know? Have you been there?

I was only inside the once. I was twenty-one years old. Five years out of school, helping run the business. Three of those years Dad was alive, and he had things organized. He was a big name in south-east London. All through my childhood, people would say, "You're Terry Starr's kid, aren't you? You look just like him —another terror!" and they'd laugh. Kids at school knew him too. I don't know if there really are kids who taunt "My Dad can whip your Dad", but nobody said it to me.

I came out of school, and it was the same. Because people respected my Dad, they looked up to me. Don't get me wrong. I ain't one of those rich men's kids who found life too easy. I ain't soft. I didn't take a free ride.

He was grooming me to help him. I knew how to run the club. I knew who was important to know. As soon as I was into long trousers I was tested several times. I passed.

Then he died on us. It was a Saturday afternoon, up at the Den.

Millwall scored, and Dad had a heart attack. Yeah, it's funny, ain't it, dying like that? Millwall didn't score often.

So that's it, you're thinking. Dad pops off, and the kid can't cope. Well, it ain't that simple. Mainly because you haven't met Ma. Now, there are mothers I know who stay home washing dishes. She wasn't like that. She was Dad's business partner. He brought the business in, set up the deals. She handled the money.

When he'd been cremated, she took over the club. The Parrot it was called, down in New Cross. You've probably heard of it. It was a useful place to meet people, to keep in touch. It had the right atmosphere. That ain't just *my* view—a kid in his teens don't know nothing—it was generally understood. We had a few villains in—well, you would, round our way—but they just used the place for drinking in, like it was their local. I guess many people thought Dad was a villain too. He looked like one—like I do. But he was straight enough. Like I was. At the time.

One of the things he did do was he kept trouble out. A place like that, you know how it is: villains want to take it over. They don't necessarily want to own it, just act as though they do. Like it's part of their empire. The trouble with that, of course, is that only one gang can do it. A club can't have two emperors. Dad kept that kind of trouble from arising. But he didn't show us how. I suppose he'd have got round to it, in time.

So Ma started running the place, and I helped out. For the first year, she held it together. She was popular. She knew the job. She'd been Terry Starr's wife.

But somehow, because he wasn't behind her, people didn't treat her the same. They thought she wouldn't manage on her own. And once you think a thing like that, you make it happen. Reputations are what people give you.

In fact, it always had been her who ran the place. She had the business brain. But no one knew that. Dad was the front, the salesman, the one the customers see.

Then the trouble started. Several gangs wanted to treat the club as their own exclusive property. Things got out of hand. The atmosphere darkened. Ma waded into those conflicts with as much steel as Terry ever had—perhaps more—but they didn't accept her. If he'd been alive—if he'd come out, big, wide and grinning

—things might have cooled. "You're the guv'nor," they'd have said. He was no tougher than she was, but they'd have listened to him.

Some of them listened to me. I looked like him. I was the man there, even then. But you have to be realistic. I wasn't Terry. I was a kid.

Then they leant on us.

This is where Ma and I have our relationship. We talked things through in every detail, like business partners, mother and son. We fought them together. And we lost.

It wasn't the big boys who beat us. It was the leftover stub of the Richardson gang. They made an ultimatum. Either we sold them the club at their price, or they'd tear it down.

We asked for time. They wouldn't give it.

There was a day around then when me and Ma had our one real argument. We stayed up half the night. I wanted to ask around for help. She said we should brazen it out. I said there were guys I knew in Deptford could destroy those Richardsons and would welcome the chance. She said we'd be beholden. I said we had to ally ourselves with someone, and it was better we chose who our friends would be.

We didn't agree.

Next day was one of those you creep through, waiting for the unknown to happen. And because it's unknown, the dread worsens with every hour. We ended up rabbits in the furrow, waiting for the fox to strike. We had stopped resisting.

So when the Richardsons blew the front of the club out, Ma was relieved. She'd passed the crisis, and survived. It wasn't as bad as she had feared. But me, I was twenty-one now. I'd been kept out of the limelight too long. I wasn't ready to curl up and give in.

I also believed that you strike while the iron is hot.

The Richardsons lived in a 1960s ranch-type construction in Blackheath—the sort of place people boast they built it them-selves. By which they mean they have friends in the building trade who persuaded them they wouldn't need an architect.

The house was an overgrown bungalow that had kept on extending. Spurs stuck out all over. Maybe if you looked down on it from an air balloon you'd see it was shaped like a swastika. They were that kind of people.

One end of the ponderosa was where they ate and watched television. The other end, they slept. I don't know what happened in between.

The night I went there was starless and dry. All day I had expected it to rain. At two in the morning I slipped over their back wall and came up on the house in the deeper shadow of the trees.

That first time I came slowest. I crept up between the trees clutching Dad's old army pistol—the one that got me three extra years in Pentonville. I felt like a bit player in a cowboy film, stalking the Indians. But I didn't need the gun. There were no dogs in the garden, and by that time of night the Richardsons were long asleep. So after that I kept the gun in my pocket. I made the journey three times.

By this time I had hauled a dozen gallons of petrol across their lawn. I worked at the bedroom end, and the Richardsons stayed asleep. Five of the six cans I placed hard against the wall. I emptied the other and sloshed it around. Then I dribbled a twenty-metre trail, and quickly, before it could dry out, I lit it.

It burned fast. I had expected the flame to run along the grass as if on a fuse. Instead, the whole damn trail lit up at the same moment. As if a floodlight had switched on, the sudden sheet of flame blazed against the wall. There was a pause. Then the five cans exploded.

I thought they'd go bang. But they made a loud whoosh. The whole side of the house flared up and dripped with flame.

As I ran back down the garden, I thought Dad would be proud of me.

I am standing in the room where he died. This was their room. For a year afterwards, Ma slept in the spare. But we never shut the door on the old one. We didn't try to block it out. Then, finally, what with one thing and another—relatives staying, that sort of thing—she moved back into their original front room. It seemed right.

She is propped up on a barrage of pillows. A bible has dropped from her hands on to the floor. I pick it up, and uncrease the page.

Ma reaches for it. She cuddles the book to her breast, like it was a hot-water bottle cooling down. She never had religion when I went into jail. Now it is part of her life.

As I sit on her bed and go through arrangements for when I'm away, she nods and says, "Yes dear." Little sinks in. If she was half the woman she used to be, she would argue, just for practice. But talking helps me check I haven't forgotten anything, and she likes a background noise. It helps her stay awake.

I tell her that there will always be a nurse on hand. I tell her I will phone every night. With her eyes closed, she slumps into her pillows. She breathes shallowly. This is one of her good times.

"A week is no time at all," I say.

"God will look after you."

I rearrange the blankets. The nurse has tucked them in too tight. Pieces of medical paraphernalia have invaded Ma's room. On the bedside cupboard glint shining steel and white porcelain. On the dressing table there is more. In front of the mirror, a sputum bowl with a steel spoon inside stands beside the silver-plated hair-brushes that April bought her. Ma can't use the brushes now—her hair is too fine. I should throw those brushes away.

They were the first present April bought her, that Christmas seven years ago. Ma used them every day. She said that if April could buy her something even half as nice next Christmas, she'd use that every day too. We both knew that April would be around the next Christmas.

By June, April and I were engaged. Ma protested that we were too young, but really she was pleased as Punch. It's not often that a mother and son can agree on his girl.

So we were both disappointed.

Once, when Ma came to visit me, she said she'd always known April was flighty. I didn't answer. We stopped talking about her. It was like April never had lived.

But in your cell at night you remember. Everyone in there has a lover outside who grows more perfect with every passing day. Sometimes you'll curse them. Sometimes you'll boast. Sometimes you'll want them. That's when it hurts.

When I came out last January, I thought of looking for her. I could find where she lived. But there was no point. By then she had been married two years. She wouldn't want reminding of me. At that time, it was one of the few wise decisions I made.

The *only* wise decisions I made were in those first three months while I tried to go straight. It never was gonna be easy. Maybe if it had been just me, on my own, I could have made it. But I wasn't on my own. I had Ma.

She was still on her feet then. In the last few months of my sentence, when she missed some visits, I blamed it on winter. Her bed-ridden state has developed only in these last three months, since she came out of hospital. All spring, before they called her in, I watched her deteriorate. She was wasting away.

We got free medical care, of course, and other assistance. But you can't live like that. This is Terry Starr's wife—my mother. She can't end her days like she's no one.

So now it is down to me. I must find money to ease her through these weeks of pain. I can't be particular how I earn it.

Gottfleisch knows that.

3

"Trust me, dear boy," purrs Gottfleisch. "It's the easiest money you'll ever earn."

He leans back against the ebonized upright of his chair, patting a napkin against his soft lips. "I have the highest expectations of you, Mickey."

This is the first time we've eaten together. It's the first time I've spent more than ten minutes with him. Up to now, he's made only brief appearances to give me instructions. Now he is welcoming me into the bosom of his organization. I should be flattered.

The smile moves a lot of flesh, but does not reach his eyes. All it does is cause his fat cheeks to swell up and create new folds of skin for his small blue eyes to drown in. His dark hair has been curled and lightly oiled, and his face looks as if several times a day he has it patted with warm towels. From his double chin to the base of his neck, deep folds of skin melt around the size 18 collar of his shirt. He wears a broad striped suit and a florid tie. From the breast pocket blooms a matching hankie. He weighs at least two-forty pounds.

A passing waiter glances round Gottfleisch's bulging frame to see if he has finished. He has not. It's an easy mistake to make. Gottfleisch looks the sort of eater who doesn't sit back from his plate till he is through. They should know him better.

This is that dark little French restaurant near the Greenwich Maritime. For Gottfleisch it is home territory. As he steamed in from the street he warbled, "This is my favourite port of call. The best sauces in London." The waiters simpered. They may have believed him. But I bet he says that to all the boys.

He was late, of course. I knew he would be. I had to wait ten minutes for him at the table, chewing my way through a packet of breadsticks.

Gottfleisch had hardly sunk on to his chair before he ordered *moules marinière*: a tureen of hot cream congested with mussel shells. He tucks a napkin in his collar to protect his beautiful shirt and tie, and absorbs his food with spoon and fingers. The spoon is for soup, the fingers for mussels. He uses one of the empty mussel shells to scoop flesh from the full ones, he raises the shell like a jam spoon to his open mouth, and he snuffles the meat down like a bird gulping breadcrumbs. He could drink the soup from a shell, except a spoon is bigger. On his side-plate he builds a neat stack of empties. They wobble in a thin puddle of cream.

I have a grapefruit.

Until he has finished, we don't say much. Then he beams me an oily great whale-smile as if he really does like me, and he sloshes more Muscadet into our chalices. They're the size of flower vases. The way Gottfleisch breathes in the aroma, you'd think they had the flowers in them. He sniffs so hard he could take wine in through his nose.

The restaurant is handy for him—just ten minutes' waddle across Greenwich Park. He lives in a mock-timbered mansion, stacked high with antiques and works of art. He deals in them. The few times I've been there it's like visiting a shop: each time you go, the merchandise changes. You can't tell which is furniture and which is stock.

While the waiter removes the plates, we act like we're not here for any reason other than eating French food. Gottfleisch sprawls across the back of his chair and makes small talk with the waiter.

I stay out of it.

When I've cut into my steak and Gottfleisch has burst the crust of his hot fish pie, we get down to business. Some business. I listen calmly, but that's because I've had time to get used to it. If Gottfleisch was springing this on me today, the steak would turn to leather in my mouth. But it is three months since he first told me. "Pop over on the quiet," he said. "Pick it up. Smuggle it back." From Russia.

Russia. It couldn't be Amsterdam. It couldn't be Paris. It couldn't be somewhere easy to get to, easy to leave. No. Not on the money he was offering. It couldn't be easy. Now he hands me my ticket and a packet of assorted documents. He writes a phone number on the wallet.

"His name is Kaplan, Leonid Kaplan. Be careful how you handle him."

"Tough, is he?"

Gottfleisch folds his flabby face into that shape he believes to be a disarming smile. "Not as tough as you, dear boy. That's why I'm sending you. But don't take him for granted. There's more to friend Kaplan than appears on the surface. He has set up a big deal here, Mickey."

"What is he—a bent party official?"

Gottfleisch pauses, his next forkful of hot fish pie steaming in mid-air. "Oh no, dear boy. He's a crook."

He swallows the fish.

"So I mustn't trust him?"

"Of course you can't trust him. Two million dollars is at stake. To set up a deal like this, Kaplan must be powerful. He will have influential friends. That's always such a worry in Russia, don't you think?"

He has everything organized. The amount of detail he has about the place, he ought to go himself. He's the most qualified. But he sends me.

I go as a tourist. Right back at the beginning, as soon as he'd asked me, Gottfleisch booked my ticket. He said that most people who go to Russia go on a package tour. Only a minority go on business. The Russians shouldn't think I'm on business, so I go tourist class. I'll be there for seven days: Saturday to Saturday.

When Gottfleisch offered me the job, I behaved as if three months' warning was customary. "To cover those three long months," I said hopefully, "I'll need some expenses."

And I got them. So I'm not complaining.

Three months with a dribble of income was worth having. It topped up my unemployment money. Gottfleisch, of course, said it was better that I did not stand idle, and he would find small jobs for me. But as I told you, small jobs worry me as much as big ones. Always they involve risk, or something dirty—like the collection job on Calvin. He was a friend of mine once.

You need a minimum of three months to get organized for Russia—fixing visas, tickets, a seat on the right tour. Three months for Ivan to do his paperwork. He must be dyslexic. But because Gottfleisch wanted me on a package, I went along with the system. A tourist, one of the crowd.

Five years in the cooler has made me cautious. It taught me you don't just leap into things—you think about them and go prepared. Not like when I did the Richardsons'. From that little escapade I learnt that when you go set a fireball on someone's house, you do not drive around there in your own car. You do not stop to admire the blaze. You do not dawdle on the way home.

I am older now. I would not try that kind of adolescent stunt again. I would not carry a gun that I was not gonna use. Though I do like to go prepared.

I asked Gottfleisch to invest in my education. A crash course in a Russian language lab, I said, would only cost a few hundred pounds. I'd get eight hours a day wearing headphones. Eight hours a day shaking off headaches. Eight hours in bed trying to sleep.

You know Gottfleisch. "Buy a home-study course, dear boy." So I did. I picked one up secondhand—knocked off, pirated, at fifteen quid, no questions asked. I made my own language lab at home. I did two stints a day, for two hours a time. Four hours a day, six days a week. In three months, I learnt enough.

Gottfleisch is saying now how much he admires me for doing it. He puts his fork into a profiterole and says I'm a promising young man. "We can go far together, you and I, Mickey. I need someone to handle the more personal parts of my business. You have an enviable reputation. You're a bright lad cheated of his vocation. But don't worry—" Here he leans across the creamy ruins of his chocolate pudding and pats me on the hand. "We'll build you up again, Mickey. This could be the start of a brand new life."

I grunt, and remove his hand.

LENINGRAD

4

By local time it is midnight. To us it is nine p.m. Already Leningrad airport is deserted. We are the last flight in, and everyone has gone home.

We shamble into queues for Immigration: three queues, at three cubicles. Inside each glass box sits a uniformed youngster staring blankly at our papers. This is where I expected to see my first formidable Russian, guarding entry to the Soviet Union. But these are kids—two boys and a girl. The old hands must have gone, leaving the kids to be last ones home. They can practise their English. They can read our Roman alphabet. Maybe Gottfleisch had something: we are only tourists, we don't matter.

But the trainees take their time. Four minutes with each of us. There is a routine to be gone through, and the kids will do it right. I watch them. I want to learn as much about their system as I can. It could be useful on the way back.

Leningrad airport is like a bus station late at night. Beyond this barrier is a dark empty hall, dark because it's empty. There is no point wasting light when all the folks have gone home.

Signposting is minimal, in English and Russian, with no other languages. In the whole building there are just two illuminated advertisements: one for Soviet jewellery, one for Pepsi Cola.

When I come to the head of the queue, I slide my passport across the cubicle shelf through the hole in the glass panel. The boy's pale face has high Slav cheekbones. He has a mid-Seventies haircut. When he holds out his hand he smiles shyly.

I slide through the rest of my papers—the visa, the ticket, the customs declaration. He reads every one. After studying our alien alphabet for two minutes, he glances up to the decal metre rule stuck on to the glass panel between us. He reads my height off it and compares it against that written in my passport. Satisfied, he carefully frames his mouth round one of his set of rehearsed questions in English. Each visitor is asked one question, to see if we remember what is written in our passport, to see if we remember who we are.

Listen Ivan, if there is one person who will have this off by heart it is the one whose papers are false. He'll know his date and place of birth, his height, his visible scars, his astrological star-sign. He'll even know his goddam passport number. He could chant them in his sleep.

Ivan doesn't realize that. He looks to see if my tired face looks like the tiny mugshot in my passport. It doesn't. The photograph makes me look like a startled monkey. But Ivan thinks it a fair likeness, and moves on to ask his test question. I wait for it.

"What is your name?"

I can handle that one. "Michael Starr."

His eyes drop to my visa, where my name is conveniently retyped in Cyrillic. "Is good," he says. He seems relieved. He bundles my papers back together and slides them through the hole. "Enjoy holiday," he says, and he lets me through. I am inside the Soviet Union.

It was simple enough. They say it's worse on the Costa Brava. But not shown on my papers is where I spent my last summer holiday. Nor the four holidays before. If Ivan had seen the word Pentonville I'd have been out on the next flight home.

After Immigration I wait in the gloomy hall with the tour party while the rest come through. Already we are used to waiting. To fly Aeroflot we had to be at Gatwick airport an extra hour early. There were no special security checks—just the waiting. This is my first flight abroad for seven years, so maybe I'm out of touch. It makes you wonder why Gottfleisch chose me. I am not what you'd call a seasoned traveller. All that stuff about my reputation, that's all guff. That ain't why he chose me. He's paying me a lot of money because there's a damn good chance I might get caught.

As we wait at the edge of the darkened hall beyond Immigration, there are no signs to Baggage Reclaim. There are no signs to anywhere at all. But we have two Intourist couriers waiting on the concourse. One is tall, lean, with cropped hair, and wears the sort of dress my mother threw away years ago. The other is a medium-tall bouncy brunette who wears the sort of dress no one throws away.

The tall thin one carries a plastic bag. In the bottom are our room tickets. When we get these we will learn for the first time which hotel we are staying in. Each ticket has someone's name on it, and comes in duplicate. One is for the courier, one is for us. In exchange for the tickets she takes our passports. She slips her duplicate inside each one and piles them on the floor. I gaze at the mound of British passports dumped on the concrete. Saying goodbye to them here is like seeing someone walk off with the key to your cell.

There's a problem. At midnight there is always a problem. Ours is a bunch of Irish school-teachers, most of whom are single and are sharing double rooms. Between themselves, the travel agent and Intourist, they have screwed the accommodation. There are married couples separated, spinster ladies with single men, seven people name of Kelly, and a bachelor in with a nun. The English suggest they sort it out on the bus. But the clan are led by a wild-eyed Celtic chaotic who comes alive when the moon is high. He grabs the courier's tickets and starts calling out the names. "Is that Cleary or O'Leary and who is B. McGuire?"

He stands grinning on the concrete, with tickets falling from his fists. Female teachers start on tales of McGuires that they have known, and the lanky courier demands her tickets back. An old lady trips over the heap of passports, and a little toddler cries.

At a quarter to two we get on the bus. In the UK it's only a quarter to eleven, but to us it feels like Russian time. We acclimatize fast.

The bus chugs out of the airport, and we stare into the gloom. We are seeing Russia for the first time. We are behind the Iron Curtain.

At two on a Sunday morning, Leningrad suburbs look like anywhere. Fading street-lamps, empty roads, sleeping windows. Shops and flats are closed for the night. A small gaggle of men cluster on a street corner, the last remains of Saturday night. Beside them, a police car has paused at the kerb. There's no trouble. They're just talking.

*

31

Within the last hour it has rained. Roads glisten in the grey light. This is the midsummer season of the White Nights when the sun never fully sets. While we are here, it will never be truly dark.

Our coach glides the whole three-mile length of Nevsky Prospekt, Leningrad's empty main parade: closed shops and public buildings, a metro every mile, tramlines down the centre, tramwires drooping overhead. At the far end, our hotel overlooks the River Neva. My map shows the Neva twisting through the city, dividing round islands, broadening and closing. By the hotel in the dusk it is wide and brown.

The Moskva Hotel is a long concrete crescent running off the drab Aleksander Nevsky Square, set across from an old monastery that bears his name. As the coach slows, we can see only the gateway to its parkland gardens.

On the hotel forecourt we climb out of the coaches and congregate like schoolkids. Hardly bothering to glance around us in the dusk, we slouch through a single glass door on to the dark marble floor of an inner lobby. We wait for our cases to be unloaded from the bus. They have gone astray.

I drift across to read the hotel noticeboard. "Visitors should take responsibility for valuables. Visitors should beware of criminals and alcoholics. Visitors should not walk in the streets after dark in groups of less than three." It sounds like home.

This is how I imagined Russia: slow and inefficient. But Gottfleisch said it would be different. It won't be like you expected, he said, it's opened up. Less of the KGB and secret police. More opportunities to trade. That's how he sees it. Well, Russia may look safe and friendly from a thousand miles away, but I notice he doesn't come himself.

The courier Olga—the tall thin one—calls us together. She looks harassed. We gather round while she breaks the news. "Some rooms are not ready because German visitors have not moved out." Groans. "Unfortunately—" More groans. "Unfortunately their flight today was not possible."

She explains that the group should have flown down to Samarkand. But another party has come up from there, leaving half their number behind, smitten with Black Mouth Disease. Whatever that is. The ill ones are tucked up in bed in central Asia, occupying rooms the Germans should have flown down to. So some of the Germans have to stay over in Leningrad, keeping their original rooms. We remain in the lobby because no one knows which rooms are which. Some of us can stay here. Some will move to the Hotel Astoria.

"What about our suitcases?"

"Who has got to move?"

"When will we know?"

Olga raises her hand like a cop on traffic duty. "It will not be long. I come back."

It will not be long. She returns to the Intourist desk and mutters in Russian to a woman in epaulettes. We mutter in English to each other. A kid starts to grizzle. Minutes slowly pass.

Later, when I draw the curtains on my bedroom window, they don't meet in the middle. The material is thin and unlined, with a floral pattern the rest of us abandoned in the Fifties. They should be a great help. In these White Nights, when the sun never sets, you can stay awake all night if you want to. With those curtains, I may have no choice.

Beside the bed is a badly printed card saying the staff want my stay to be memorable. There are no pictures on the wall, no welcoming bowl of fruit. The wallpaper is formal, the chipboard sombre brown. The TV works in black and white, and its plug is faulty. The bathroom washbasin has no plug at all. When I turn on the taps I get brown water: hot and cold. We were told on the bus not to drink it. It's unsafe. This is the second city of one of the world's two superpowers, and they can't supply clean water.

A knock at the door.

At three in the morning it is not what I expect to hear. So I edge across the bedroom and ask like an old lady who it is. He grunts in Russian. I open up.

He is a porter. He stands outside in the corridor with cases piled on a trolley. He looks at me. We both do nothing. Then I remember that this is a self-service country. I pull my case off the pile and swing it into the room. He trundles off. In Russia you carry your own bag. But you don't pay a tip.

5

In the first floor dining-hall we are eight to a table. Our places are fixed for the time we are here. There is no menu, because there is no choice. We start with brown and white bread, slices of limp cheese, and beakers of buttermilk which nobody drinks because it smells like the cheese. So we drink mineral water, which also does not smell good. They bring coffee. They bring tea. Then they bring the porridge. Conversation falters. Collective eating and organized tours could make this an over-communal holiday. The kind of people who can afford to come here will not like fixed company at fixed tables. They came to see communism, not to join in.

At my table are three couples and two singles. There is a recently wed couple around my age. When they get home they will start the first baby, because they're at the age when raising families is the right thing to do. There is an unaffected older couple, easy to get along with. There's a pair of glum teachers from Chiswick, and a Scotsman. He's twenty-three. Before coming out yesterday, he had a last-minute flight change, so had to fly Glasgow to Gatwick. Four hundred miles.

"Aye, it's typical," Sammy says. "I booked last January, and in June they cannae fit me on the flight. Would you credit it?"

I would. One look at him shows he is the sort that the unlikely happens to. He has red hair, cut in a shaggy outgrown crewcut. His flesh is pockmarked, and where it isn't sprinkled with freckles the untouched skin is white as paper. He sits eating breakfast wearing a "David Bowie Glass Spider Tour" teeshirt, and he peers across at me through metal-framed round glasses. You know that either he's a rock musician or he works in computers. I ask, and he works in computers.

I can play the tourist too. For our first morning I will tag along on the city tour to get my bearings.

We come out on to the damp pavement, and stand relaxed in the cool air. Clouds are clearing. A wet northern sun hangs pale and high in the grey-blue sky. Puddles shrink around our feet. The two couriers, Olga and Natalia, shepherd us on to buses. Though it's Sunday, there is a schedule. The Intourist machine has started.

The couriers take a coach each. I choose Natalia's because she is the pretty one, and even in Russia you never know. She follows us into the coach, picks up the mike, and introduces herself. I try to catch her eye but don't succeed. We move off. Over the PA, Natalia's voice is deep and husky. She drones to us about who built which building when, and what it's used for now, and whether Lenin ever went there or worked there or just gave his name to it, and I switch off to watch the view. I stare through coach windows at enormous empty streets.

We don't see any shops. Or bars. Or cinemas. Yet they say there are more cinemas in Russia than anywhere else in the world. We see a kind of shut-down Scandinavian suburb: grey and beige buildings, municipal, monumental, grand but cheerless. No bright posters. No flowers. No displays in the windows.

Leningrad stands on an icy reclaimed swamp where the river Neva splinters and empties into the freezing Gulf of Finland. Back when Peter the Great created this place—Saint Petersburg, as it was then—thousands of its builders drowned, caught fevers, or froze to death. They built a Venice in the north—the same classical style, the same blend of river and stone. And while Venice now decays and sinks into the sea, Leningrad stands preserved above the ice.

The Neva splits and twists, goes back on itself and rejoins. Canals and little rivers dart through the town. In winter the waters will freeze over, but now in June they are choppy and blue, sparkling in the weak sunlight.

Leningrad is made of islands, and in the heart of the city where the Neva is at its widest, we cross on to one of the smallest. It is here, Natalia tells us, that the city began: here on tiny Hare Island, smothered by the Peter and Paul Fortress. In this tourist-trodden stockade, Peter the Great ate wild boar and venison while his labourers died. After his own death the fortress became a prison. Natalia lists its famous prisoners: Dostoevsky, Gorky, Lenin's

35

older brother. I hear no one with the name of Starr. In the pale summer sunlight the place looks prettier than Pentonville.

Then she tells of the day Dostoevsky was led out blindfold before a firing squad. He stood sightless in this very yard, and heard the rifles load. In the chill morning air he heard orders barked. Only at the last second did they tell him his sentence was commuted. Instead he was exiled for four years in Siberia. Followed by four more in the army. Russians always were bastards for punishment: the communists didn't invent it.

These are stories any city would tell. These are their attractions, their tourist sights. Look at them through the windows of your coach. But on Aptekarsky Island, Natalia has us out again on to the breezy waterside. We should not miss this, she says.

The squat grey cruiser has three stovepipe funnels, and is moored where the Neva divides to encircle Aptekarsky. Natalia tells us that this is *not* the Battleship *Potemkin*. It is the *Aurora*, the hulk which in October 1917 fired the symbolic first shot to launch the Bolshevik attack on the Winter Palace. It means a lot to her. She skips about the quayside in a short navy skirt and white blouse, like a schoolmistress taking outdoor class. Her dark hair is scraped into a bun, and on one side a single long brown wisp has fallen free, to dance in the breeze against her cheek.

She brings a group of old ladies over beside me at the water's edge to point out the sights. They look where she is pointing. I look at her arm nestling in the fabric of her blouse. Inside the white cotton sleeve she has skin brown as a ginger biscuit. Her shirt collar is open. As she points across the river, her breasts move inside the blouse and press against the buttons.

"Leningrad Hotel." She nods towards a huge concrete slab crushing the life out of the opposite riverbank. "Seventeen storeys. In front is a pool where lives the spirit of Neva. We cannot see her."

She slips back into her commentary. She has a beautiful skin. Not that over-smooth sheen women get from pancake make-up, but more open—the texture of raw silk. She has brown eyes beneath dark hair, and tiny gold studs, star-shaped, in each ear. When she stops talking, she tilts her head and smiles at me. She just asked me something.

"I'm sorry," I say. "I didn't catch that."

She shrugs. "I thought you were listening."

She turns back to the old ladies and moves away. An Irish spinster crooks her eyebrow at me and grins. "You have to pay attention," she says. "You've upset her now."

Women. They get their claws into you, dig in their nails. They maul you about. I was lucky that April ditched me. I'm too young to settle down. This Russian needn't think she's special. She is not for me.

Don't get me wrong. I'm not one of those who doesn't like women. I love women, some of them. Love them. I'm no virgin. I have *been* with women since I came out. I have tried them. But they gotta not keep needling me because I don't act like the heroes in their magazines. Because I don't act all dark and smouldering, then surprise them with gifts of flowers. Dark and smouldering I can manage, but not flowers. They're pointless. They sit in a pot a day or two, then die there. There's no sense in it.

So this Natalia can climb back on her bus and talk to old ladies. I only looked at her, for Christ's sake. It didn't mean a thing.

6

Back in the hotel for our first lunch. "A wee Russian salad," predicts Sammy. But we get caviar. It's only the cheap red stuff—glistening orange globules on a slice of hard-boiled egg. But it's caviar. Some folk screw up their noses, but I shrug and eat three helpings. Then they grind out the rest of the meal: a tureen of mushroom soup, followed by slices of breaded fish, a cakestand loaded with ice-cream and raspberry sauce. Coffee.

Lined up along the centre of the table are bottles of sparkling orange juice and plain Russian mineral water. The orange tastes like orange, but the mineral water tastes like yesterday's soda laced with disinfectant.

I stick to coffee.

Chairs scrape, people rise, and it's time for the afternoon tour. The Summer Palace, the Lenin Museum and the Field of Mars. A trip I'm gonna miss.

While the tourists trundle into their next bus, I have a wash in my room. In my bathroom mirror I see a tousled guy in an open-necked shirt who looks like he'll spend Sunday afternoon in the garden. I should put on a tie and smarten up. But Leningrad is a city where everybody dresses down. I guess the idea is that this is a workers' state, so they're all comfortable in their working clothes. Back in Deptford, when we have a day off, we dress up for it, we enjoy ourselves. And we're working-class, Ivan, ask anyone.

I grin at my reflection, and the sad-looking guy grins back. He ain't convincing. This is a face has lost the art of smiling. It has aged in the last six years.

Six years. Five and a bit in the cooler, six months outside. Sometimes I think the six months out of prison have been longer than the five years before. I did try to go straight in those months. I ain't a natural criminal. I tried working for myself, but the police

38

kept hassling. I took job interviews. "What have you been doing these last five years?"

Try explaining that away. You can say you were working casual. You can say you were out the country. But they can tell. The only people who did offer me jobs were the kind of people I was trying to avoid. They came round fast enough. "Hallo Mickey," they'd say. "Want to earn some easy cash? Expect you could use it, things being the way they are."

Each time they asked, I refused. I said I was going straight. Each time I said it, they laughed.

So I had no money, and Ma was sick. She'd been fit when I went in, but you've seen the way she is now. She needs looking after. It costs money. I needed a fresh start, which also costs money. I didn't know what to do. Going straight meant going hungry. It meant watching Ma shivering in the house.

I got a phone call. Would I come and meet a man called Gottfleisch? He might have a job for me. A job that paid real money.

And here I am.

I stroll out the hotel looking anonymous, and head down a Russian pavement for the first time on my own. At the street corner is a metro station. I pass it. In Aleksander Square the buildings are sullen. Everywhere's shut. I continue through, into the bottom of the long shopping street. It gets busier the further I walk. Trolleys clank along the middle of the road, and old cars pass either side. Among the thickening crowd, a boy stops in front of me. He wears a teeshirt, and has short fair hair.

"You like to change some money?"

I look surprised.

"You change sterling with me? I give you roubles. Good rate."

I shake my head curtly, and walk by. I don't look back. I ain't falling for that. I ain't being sent back home for the sake of five fast tenners. I'm staying clean.

An hour later in Palace Square I see her standing among tourists craning their necks at the foot of the 150-foot Aleksander Column.

With a thousand other people here, queuing, strolling, adjusting their cameras, it is amazing that I notice her at all.

"Hallo," I say.

Natalia gives me the half-second half-smile that a shop girl gives her next customer. Her brown eyes flick away across the square. "Hallo," she echoes.

I wonder why I bother. Then I touch her elbow. "Shouldn't you be working?"

"Is my half-day off." But her hair is still tight in its bun.

"So you missed the museum of whatever it was?"

"Lenin Museum. Field of Mars. Is near to here."

"Oh."

We stand in silence for a while, stunned by the brilliance of our conversation. We're so close we're almost touching. I can feel the warmth coming off her body, I can feel her breathing. "I must go now," she says, turning away. I suggest that maybe we could wander round together.

"I do not think so." The shop-girl's smile again, the one for when the customer tries to get fresh. She says, "Continue where you were going."

"That wasn't anywhere. We could have a coffee."

"Where?" She sniffs, and waves her hand contemptuously round the square.

"You're the guide. Where do you suggest?"

"This is not Britain. We do not have coffee bars. Please, you go where you were going."

"We can walk there together."

"I return to Intourist Office. I am still working. Goodbye, Mr Starr."

She swings her hips away across the grey cobbles, and I watch her go. When she reaches the corner of the vast square, she glances back. Then she continues down the road and disappears.

At least she knew my name.

Back in my hotel bedroom, I pick up the phone. This could take a while. I dial the switchboard. After three rings a woman answers. I speak in English. "I want to phone England."

"One moment please." A pause, then a man cuts in and says,

"You like to telephone England? What number please?" I give it to him. "And *your* number?"

He wants my room number. That's the system. They bill it straight to your room. "We call you back in a little while." He cuts off. I put down the phone.

Now I can have a bath while they place the call. I imagine a thousand miles of cable crawling out of Russia into Estonia, Latvia, Lithuania, clambering over the border into Poland, whipping off across both Germanies, through Belgium, under the Channel, up the Essex mudflats on to UK mainland, along the Thames into the heart of London, diverting south of the river, picking its way for the last part of its journey into the back streets of Deptford, and finally running up the garden path into number 24. Ring, ring. Anybody home?

But before it gets there, my call will need clearance to leave Leningrad, permission to cross each border. The whole damn process may take a couple of hours. That's according to the guidebook.

So I go and run that bath.

You will know without my telling you that if you sit waiting for the phone to ring, it does not. And if you sink into a hot bath, it does.

So I leap up out the water, splashing and slipping as if I'd just fallen in, grab a skimpy towel and paddle across the floor. When I pick up the receiver, I drip water on the bed.

"Your call to England. We are connecting you. Go ahead please."

"Hallo?" I pant.

"Hallo?" She is English. Whoever *she* is.

"Can I speak to Mrs Starr?"

"Who is that calling?"

"Mickey. Her son."

"Hello, Mr Starr. She's sleeping, I'm afraid."

"Sleeping?"

"Having a nap."

"But it's lunchtime."

"It's best not to wake her."

"Is she all right?"

41

"Perfectly."

"So why is she sleeping?"

"She's just sleeping."

"Oh."

"I'll tell her you called, shall I?"

"Do that."

"She will be pleased. I'll tell her."

"Yeah. Is she really all right?"

"Really. There's nothing to worry about. Do you want to leave a message?"

"No. I'll phone again."

"Goodbye, Mr Starr."

"Goodbye, Miss—What's your name, by the way?"

The line is dead.

I put the phone down and look at my feet. They are pressing into a swamp of carpet, making dents as if I'm standing in wet sand.

I return to the bathroom. The water has cooled. I slide under, up to my chin. I find the soap.

Sleeping.

I phoned now deliberately, because with English time being three hours behind, it is lunchtime there. So why is she sleeping? This is Sunday. Sunday she should be fine. I won't phone tomorrow, because Monday is radiotherapy and she's useless after that.

The nurse sounded different. I didn't recognize her voice. She must be a new one from the agency that Gottfleisch recommended. We don't have medical insurance, because we couldn't afford it and I didn't believe in it. All those private wards, clinics, stinking-rich consultants—they are not for ordinary people. They are not for us. Around our way, if you get sick you call the doctor. If he says you need it, you go to hospital. He decides according to whether you need it, not if you can afford it. Not on whether you paid the premiums. We're supposed to have a National Health Service. National, you know? For everybody.

I came out of prison like Rip Van Winkle, and found there wasn't a National Health Service any more. All that was left was a National Sick Scheme. What we Starrs got from the National Sick Scheme was hot stuffy waiting rooms and cheap hard chairs. Cold floors and gloss-painted walls. We didn't qualify for Home Help,

42

or Meals on Wheels, or someone to help with the cleaning, because I lived at home. I could do all that.

But now that I'm off earning money, I need the nurse to keep an eye on her. She is there to hold Ma's hand. Some days Ma is worse than other days. She's bad on Mondays, and Monday nights. Come the weekend, she hardly needs anyone. It's only half the time she's bad.

"I'll tell you this," I say over supper, "I haven't seen a bar in this place yet. I wandered all over town—nothing. I come back to the hotel—nothing."

"The country's dry," scoffs Scottish Sammy. His freckles have erupted in the sun. "Ever since yon Gorbachev and his *perestroika*, alcohol has disappeared."

"Like in Prohibition."

"Aye, almost. It's like a lot of things in Russia—" His Scottish accent rolls the "R" in "Russia". "It isnae banned, it's just you cannae get it. It's no available."

"We're here for a week without a drink?"

"We can use the *Berioskas*. They sell alcohol."

They're a chain of hard-currency shops, run by the state but trading only in real money, in anything but roubles. But here in the restaurant there is not a bottle of wine in sight. My throat is dry. With all this stodgy food I need a drink.

"There'll be a way," says Sammy.

There are always ways, he says. On this afternoon's trip to the Field of Mars he was approached three times for an illegal money exchange. He would have stood out, in shades, jeans, "Glass Spider Tour" teeshirt, and four hundred quid's worth of camera draped round his neck. Lord knows what they made of his accent.

"I wasnae sure about the first one," he says. "He might have been the KGB. But I tried him out. The official rate is one for one, right? One rouble for one pound. D'you know what he was offering? Four for one."

"Four?"

"Aye, four times the going rate. Not bad, is it? But I didnae take it. Not from him."

"From someone else?"

"The next laddie offered four to one, but I argued him up to five, then did a tenner. That's fifty roubles I got, for ten. The next offered five straight away, so I said six, and he said he couldnae stretch to that. I asked how he'd get rid of the money, and he said he was saving up for a food mixer to give his wife. By that time I'd taken pity on the poor wee laddie, so I changed him five to one as a favour. Fifty roubles again."

"It beats horse racing."

"Everybody's doing it. There's an Irishwoman did fifty pounds this morning on the city tour, and she got six to one. What'll she do with three hundred roubles? She cannae take them home."

This is true. Most countries don't bother about what you take out. They search what you take in. Russia is different. Sensitive. Though with tourists, I hope, they should just go through the motions, wave us through. Pick out a few cases and examine only those. Thoroughly.

What are the odds they will pick on mine? I'm on my own. Not a family, not a couple, not a swarm of Irish teachers. On my own. A tough-looking guy with an East End accent, holidaying by himself. It might be worth looking in that big suitcase of his.

But you won't find anything there, Ivan. I have it all sussed out. Why d'you think Gottfleisch hired me—because I'm an amateur? Not after Pentonville.

I sit in the dining-hall, looking at schmoes who are amateurs. All these suburban souls who, unlike me, have been dealing in illegal currency. Doing deals in broad daylight. Trading in sterling among the crowds. And here am I, the only con among them, and *I've* done a deal with no one. All I've got is twenty roubles, bought one for one at the hotel desk. It's embarrassing.

After supper I mosey around the *Berioska* store to see what they've got. There's a liquor store, closed for stocktaking. There are wooden toys, fur wraps, trinkets and jewellery. I look at the jewellery. Maybe they've got a crucifix I could take home to Ma. But they haven't. It's all earrings, bracelets, stuff like that. I pick up an amber necklace and let the beads run through my fingers. The woman behind the counter reads her book. She doesn't try to sell to me. If I want it, I'll buy it, that's what she thinks.

I try a phrase of my Russian: *"Izvinite, skolko eto stoit?"*

She mutters the price, and I frown at her. *"Govorite, pozhalusta, medlenneye."*

She repeats it slowly, but I still can't catch it. *"Eto slishkom dorogo,"* I say, and put it down. The woman shrugs and replaces the necklace on the stand. I peer through the glass top of her counter at the pieces underneath. She loses interest. But a little portly man, pretending he's a customer, has his eye on me. He ain't a customer. He's a Russian, and I guess he's the store detective. I'm the sort he keeps an eye on. I always was.

Just to annoy him, I take a hold of another necklace. I move along the counter with it. But when I turn away to hold it up to the light, the woman puts her book down and stands up. Do I want to buy this one?

I replace it on its stand. The tubby guy still watches me. He has moved around so he appears to be studying the guidebooks, but he watches me from the corner of his eye. I stare back. Then I tire of this and leave the shop. I slouch out the front of the hotel, cross the coach-park and tramlines, and pick my way easily between light traffic to the wall by the Neva. I watch it flowing.

Then I become aware of someone standing beside me. The little portly guy is a short way off along the wall, gazing out across the water, like me.

From the look of him, you'd think that instead of being in this late low slanting light, we were standing in the midday sun. He is sweating slightly. His trousers are too tight. His shirt has become twisted in his waistband. I wait for him to speak. It isn't long.

"So you speak Russian," he begins in English.

"A little."

"Is sounding very good. So—ah—" He looks uncertain what to say. "You like our country?"

"Oh sure, very nice."

I don't know whether he is practising his English or building up to strike a deal. Maybe he is worried because I speak a little Russian. I could be a snare. He sweats some more, then takes the chance: "You want to change some English money with me?"

"No thanks."

"In hotel they give you one for one. I give five. Five roubles for

46

one pound." He licks his fleshy lips, and swallows. It looks as if swallowing reminds him he is hungry.

"No thanks," I say again. "I only change money with Intourist."

He smiles. "But they give only one for one. I give five."

"I'll keep my nose clean."

"Please?"

"I don't want to trade."

"Ah." He pauses, still dreamily watching the Neva roll by. "But you look for jewellery. You do not like what is in *Berioska*?"

"I wanted old jewellery. They didn't have what I want."

"Really? Antiques you can buy in Leningrad."

I glance round at him. He's a comfortable, middle-thirties kind of guy, who ought to be smoking a pipe. "Can I buy old crucifixes, things like that?—You know what a crucifix is?"

"Sure, I know. What do you think? Yes, you can buy, but not in *Berioska*. I know where there are such things. Hard currency, of course."

I smile. Always hard currency. Then I frown at him. "I don't mean black market, understand?"

He throws his hands wide. "Naturally. You want—ah—high quality."

"How much might a crucifix cost?"

"It depends. You pay pounds or dollars?"

"Pounds."

He thinks for a second or two, and draws closer to me. Then he shivers, as if the river air had nibbled at his ribs. "Old crucifix, yes? I think maybe from three hundred pound to three thousand a piece. I am not sure."

He squints at me, to see how I'll react. Three hundred pounds. It seems a helluva lot for a crucifix, even an antique. I want to buy Ma something decent, but I can't afford that kind of money.

He is still looking up at me. "They sound expensive," I say.

"But are very good. You like to see?"

"I might. What's the place called? You have an address?"

"I arrange. We can see now, if you like."

"Just give me the address. I'll stop by."

"Is no trouble. I arrange now."

47

"No, no, no." I take a firm but gentle hold of his elbow. "It's getting late. Shops are shut. I am not interested in doing deals on the black market."

"Is not black market." He seems genuinely indignant. He looks me straight in the eyes. Either he is checking his assessment of me, or he is trying to convince me how honest he is. "You want—how you say—genuine articles. I understand. I arrange it now. Five minutes, maybe ten. Is no problem."

"I ain't hanging around."

"I come to hotel."

"No."

"We meet in five minutes. In metro station. I phone my friend."

I can see now that he has the wrong idea. He just wants to fix up a street-corner deal.

"Forget it," I say.

"No, please." He touches my arm tentatively. Then he pulls his hand away sharply, as if my arm was hot. "Is no problem. My friend has many jewelleries."

"I bet."

"We meet in open street. Plenty people."

He is insistent. He's a flabby little guy, like I say, and he clutches my arm again, more confidently now, squeezing it like he'd squeeze a watermelon to see if it was ripe. I let him lead me to the metro. He hurries to where some telephones hang on a wall. "Two minutes," he insists. "Please wait."

I let him dial his friend. I can't hear what he says. When Tubby puts the phone back on its rest, he smiles at me and says, "Five minutes. You like a drink, yes?"

I brighten up. But when he leads us a few more metres down the road, my hopes fade. Mounted in a row on the wall are some soft-drink machines. He selects one. Each battered machine has a small recess in its front where the drinks are vended, and in each hole stands a glass, upside down. Tubby takes one, and places it over some sort of rubber paddle within the recess. From the bowels of the machine spurts a squirt of detergent to swill out the glass. Tubby transfers the disinfected glass to the drink spout, and drops three kopeks in a slot. The glass fills. He hands it to me, and moves to the neighbouring machine. While I use the first glass, the machine cannot be used. A family of four would tie up four machines for a minute and a half. I sip cautiously. It's that same sweet-sour fizzy water we ignore in the hotel dining-hall. It tastes of something but you're not sure what. Probably the detergent.

Tubby enjoys his water like it's a new kind of beer, and replaces his glass. I dash mine out in the puddle by the machine, put my glass back in its recess, and walk away. I should not be here. This is not a good idea.

He follows me into the drab square. I wonder which way I should give him the brush-off: soft or hard. "I'm sorry I troubled you," I say. "I changed my mind."

"Is no trouble."

"I don't want to buy."

"You think you buy somewhere else? My friend has best jewellery in Leningrad."

Traffic trundles by in the evening sun—ancient lorries, cheap cars, odds and ends. I turn on the kerb and shake my head. "Sorry," I say. "Some other time."

An old blue Zhiguli stops beside us. "My friend," says Tubby, and an elephant climbs out. The man is as big as an elephant anyway, only his ears are smaller and his skin is a shade less grey. His huge arm reaches towards me, like an elephant's trunk stretching for a bun. He grabs my hand and says, "How you do?"

I'm a polite kind of guy, and I say "How d'you do" back.

Tubby says, "Please step in."

"In there?"

"Please."

I shake my head. "I ain't driving off in no car."

Elephant still has hold of my hand. He doesn't want to let go. I try pulling out of his grip, but his fingers contract round my hand like quick-drying cement. I pull again. This time he seems to notice. He looks down at me as if I'd insulted him. Then he jerks me past him into the car. My shins crunch against the door sill. As I scrabble to get hold of something, another hand reaches out from inside the car, grabs my collar and hauls me inside. I struggle for three whole seconds before they push me on to the back seat. Elephant's face appears close against the front of mine. I try to head-butt him. He lands a clunk around my jaw that fills the car full of red.

It doesn't knock me out. I sit there with my jaw throbbing. It aches as if Elephant had stood on it. Some square-shaped guy is driving, and we three are in the back, squashed together like crackers in a box: me, Tubby and the Elephant. There's no point my trying to work out where this poky little Zhiguli is going, because I don't know where we are already. I wonder what usually happens when a bunch of Russian hoods bundle you off in an unmarked car. Just don't let them steal my Western clothes. I don't want to be dumped out the car in the Leningrad suburbs wearing only my Y-fronts.

Tubby is cooing some kind of apology in my ear. He says his friend was hasty. He says I shouldn't worry, because he is taking me to see his other friend who is a real nice guy. I glare at the Elephant, and he stares down his trunk at me as if he's wondering when he'll get another bun. He looks uncomfortable. He has to keep his head crooked at an angle with his chin against his collarbone, otherwise he'd stick out through the roof. I want no trouble with him. The only way you stop a guy like that is with a cannon. But he doesn't say anything. He doesn't do anything. He acts like he's forgotten I'm there; he's forgotten that he slugged me. He probably does it so often it is easy to forget. It's like breathing.

Then Tubby stops apologizing. He has said his piece. I can believe him if I want to, but it makes no difference. We drive on in silence.

We squeeze into a narrow street and pull up. Tubby opens the door. This releases the pressure so much that we all ooze out the car like foam from a burst cushion. Tubby and Elephant bundle me across the pavement and into the house. The third guy stays in the car. Indoors, the hall is about ninety feet long and lit by a forty watt bulb. Half-way down we stop at a plain door. The bell rings somewhere inside, and we wait without speaking. My jaw feels like it had a dentist's injection which wore off too soon.

When the door opens, it only moves three inches. Then it closes. A chain is released, the door re-opens, and the whole room appears.

It is the first decent room I've seen since I got here. There are soft lights and Scandinavian furniture. In the centre of a white long-pile rug stands a round little man with olive skin, sleek as a casino floor-manager. His black hair is greased so close to his skull that it looks painted on. His nose and ears lie flat against his face.

He is smiling. As he waddles forward to shake my hand, gold sparkles in his teeth. "Welcome," he says. "How are ya, buddy?"

I stand looking at him, a Russian with a Brooklyn accent. I don't hold out my hand. "The last time I shook someone's hand I nearly got it yanked off."

He raises a pencilled eyebrow to the Elephant, who mutters in Russian that I took awkward.

"Vy nichevo ne skazali emu?"

"Niet."

"He speaks Russian," Tubby says.

The little Napoleon pirouettes toward me. "We oughta speak English, as a courtesy to our guest."

His accent sounds as if he learnt it from American B-movies and is still honing up. I say nothing. The way my jaw throbs, it is the easiest way. Napoleon continues: "So, Mr—do we know ya name? Well, who cares? Why don'cha sit down?"

I still say nothing. Napoleon smiles. Unconvincingly.

"I oughta apologize for my friend's behaviour, but you were aggressive, I think. No hard feelings, eh, buddy?"

"Why am I here?"

He puts an arm around Tubby's shoulder. Tubby looks apprehensive. "My friend Vladimir thinks we can do business," Napoleon purrs.

"Business?"

"Why don'cha sit down?"

"I like standing."

"Really? That's interesting." He walks slowly round me, in-specting me head to foot like I was a slave-girl in the market. When he disappears behind me I don't twist round. If he's gonna try something, I can't stop him. So I wait. From somewhere between my shoulder-blades he whispers, "I prefer you sit down."

There are times you gotta act sensible. This is one. I slouch to my right, eyeing up the chairs. The trouble with these arty Scandinavian things is you don't know how they'll behave when

51

you sit. So I choose a conventional armchair. It turns out to be harder than it looks.

Now I am sitting while they are all standing. If it is meant to unnerve me it does not work. I look up at them, and try to ignore the pain in my jaw. I cross my legs, and smile like I am Bulldog Drummond inside the master criminal's den. "Won't you sit down too, gentlemen?"

Tubby and Elephant look to Napoleon. He picks up a tubular-steel dining chair, drags it across the white carpet, and plonks it in front of me. He sits on it backwards, so he can lean on the steel upright. He grins, flashing gold. The other two bobos shuffle their feet, and wonder where to sit.

"You are not tourist," Napoleon says.

I raise an eyebrow.

"You can talk freely. We're all friends here."

I raise the other brow.

He snaps "*Syad' te, duraki*," over his shoulder, and they scuttle for seats.

"I said he was not tourist," bleats Tubby, sitting down. "It is—ah—obvious."

Napoleon stares at me. "What kinda jewellery d'ya want?"

I consider whether I should reply. The right thing to do is either to stay silent or to get up and walk out the room. Except they are not gonna let me.

"I wanted a crucifix," I say. "One crucifix, for my mother."

Napoleon keeps his dark little eyes fixed on mine. Then he smiles, briefly. "For your mother," he says.

"Yeah, a present. She'd like a crucifix." My voice has thickened, as if Elephant had loosened some teeth.

"I can show ya crucifixes," he says. "How many d'ya want?"

"One."

"How much you pay?"

I shrug. "What price do they start?"

He speaks across my shoulder to Tubby in Russian. I can't translate it, but I get the gist. He wants to know if we are wasting his time. Tubby tries to reassure him.

Napoleon switches to English. "We think you here on business. We like to help ya. You wanna see what I got?"

I shake my head. "There's been a mistake. I'm a tourist. I'm not here to trade."

Napoleon studies me. "You have identity?" he asks.

"You sound like the KGB."

"I told ya, we're businessmen. Lemme see your wallet." He reaches out his hand.

There is no point playing coy. Not now. Either they will fix me or they will not. It is already decided.

When I pull out my wallet, they stare at it like it was black velvet and full of pearls. If a ghost slipped across the room, they would not notice.

I thumb open the popper and drop the wallet into his hand. He looks inside. He ignores the money, but examines everything else. I do not carry a credit card, since back home I would not be considered an acceptable risk. But I carry the visa we must keep with us wherever we go—the one with the photocopied pages from my passport.

"Pleased to meet ya, Mr Starr," he says. He replaces the visa in the wallet and returns it to me. I slip it back in my trouser pocket and decide he is going to let me go.

"Listen, Mr Starr, let's not play around. We can help you. You want something that's difficult to find, we find it for you. There's nothing in Leningrad you can't have, so long as you know where to look. And we know where to look. Anything you want in Leningrad, I know where it is." This is said with some pride.

I nod. He's a small-time racketeer who thinks he found a stake. I shouldn't have been soft with Tubby. It set their saliva running.

Napoleon waves his plump hand around the room. "In here is—what d'ya call it—treasure trove. Look at this place. This carpets, this curtains, this furniture—you think you can buy this in the shops? Not in Leningrad, buddy. We have American cigarettes, French perfume, alcohol. You like a drink? Vodka? Whisky? Crème de Menthe?"

"Rum and Coke."

"Whatever you like.—Vladimir!"

Tubby jumps up. In the corner is the kind of black and chrome cocktail bar that went out with Chubby Checker. Vladimir can't wait to get his hands on it. He grabs two bottles.

"Coke," I say. "Not Pepsi."

Tubby little Vladimir looks uncertain. Napoleon smiles. "There's no Coca-Cola. It's a symbol of American colonialism. Isn't that stupid? Have Pepsi."

I glance again round the room while Tubby clinks the glasses. Yeah, it's all here, it looks expensive, but . . . it ain't together, it's a hotch-potch. This is the kind of Scandinavian furniture got left behind in the saleroom. The lamps are from the Seventies, and the rugs don't match. The things are remainders: bits he couldn't sell.

Napoleon sees me studying his inventory. "Lemme show you what we got."

"I don't want to buy."

"Sure you don't."

But he shows me anyway. Most of the stuff is consumer durables for the domestic market. He also has jewellery, in silver, gold or enamel, and the few crucifixes he has look like they were made last week in Birmingham. He has icons, thinly painted on cracked wood so they look less new. But from the casual way he handles them I guess they're fakes. He has furs, which mean nothing to me. I can't tell sable from skunk.

"I can't use any of this."

"What *can* you use, Mr Starr? Anything you want, we find."

"I don't want anything."

"Maybe you're here to sell, not to buy. Is that it?"

"No."

"You're really a puzzle, you know?"

I decide to find whether I will be allowed to leave, so I stand up. "It was interesting meeting you, Mr—er—?" He doesn't react. "I'll be going now."

He stares at me flatly, looking like a badly-made Buddha anointed with the wrong kind of oil. Elephant and Tubby watch him. He says, "OK, buddy, you're free to leave. If you change your mind we talk again. You understand if I don't give ya my card?"

"Naturally." I start for the door.

"We'll drive you back to your hotel. And Mr Starr, I know I don't need to say . . ."

"I never saw you in my life."

His eyes cloud over, and he loses interest.
Elephant drives me home. We don't talk.

I suppose you think that I meet guys like Napoleon all the time?
You think I get in a lot of scrapes. You think I like getting thumped
across the jaw.

Half the honest tourists in my party have done deals to change
their money, and what did they get? Five for one. I chat to a fat guy
in the street, and get clobbered in a car. There's no justice.

In my hotel bedroom I lie on one of the two beds, holding a cold
damp flannel to the side of my jaw, trying to work out what I did
wrong. In Russia, I am outside home territory. But wherever we
go, I guess, guys like me attract the Napoleons of this world. They
can smell us. Well, for the next twenty-four hours I shall behave
myself so well my own mother wouldn't recognize me. My mother.
I should have phoned her again. But it's midnight. That's nine
o'clock in Deptford, but by the time I get a call through, she'll be
sleeping. I'll phone tomorrow. There'll be plenty of time.

This Napoleon business worries me. Here I am, keeping my
head down. I take one little peek over the parapet and blam!
Bundled into a Zhiguli. I wouldn't be seen dead in a Russian car
back home.

8

One of the old ladies turns to her husband. He's spent a life-time listening to her. "All that walking yesterday, it killed me. Especially the coming back."

"You nearly missed the bus," he says.

"I nearly missed the bus."

"Today," says Olga grimly, "we will walk slowly."

"Is it far?"

"No."

We're on the Memorial Tour. I'm stuck with Sammy and his Batman teeshirt. While he prattles about black-market currency, I wish there was a vicar I could hang out with, to keep me out of trouble.

Sammy points behind us, among the Irish. "Yon's a Mr Shady. He asked me a moment ago, but I wasnae interested."

The black marketeer wears an American teeshirt, decent jeans and white canvas shoes. He carries a black holdall round his neck, and has four Irish ladies babbling at him as if he was selling vegetables. They're probably asking seven for one.

I glance up front. Ahead of us, Olga and Natalia look studiously ahead. By the time we enter the Avenue of the Unsubdued, the deals have been done. Irishwomen are chuckling, Mr Shady has slipped away, and I don't want to hear how much profit they've made.

Soon, we walk in silence. The air is still. Immediately around us are neat lawns before walls of green trees. Out of sight now, but within the railings of this colossal cemetery, lie the anonymous mass graves of half a million Leningraders. We have seen the Museum to the War Dead, the great stone memorials, the endless granite tombstones. Now the peace and neatness of this central formal garden, the hard stone path between soft green borders, bring the dead closer to us.

At one end of the 300-yard parterre stands the towering bronze and granite Statue of The Motherland. Here at the other end burns the eternal flame, flickering steadily above a plain rectangular marble slab. Scattered across the topmost surface are five bunches of carnations, recently laid. Before the flame, oblivious to us, an old woman in black kneels and bows her head. Her lips mouth a silent prayer.

My mother knelt the same way in the crematorium chapel. She too mouthed words I couldn't hear. The old woman kneeling here today, remembering someone who died more than forty years ago, seems as stunned by death now as my mother was the day Dad died. All through the day of the funeral, people approached her hesitantly to lay hands on her, and each time they did so, she flinched. When the last one had left, when she and I remained trembling in the empty house, only then did she grieve.

The old Russian woman pushes herself up and walks away. Olga has waited for her to do so. Now she strides to the same spot where the old woman knelt, and while she tells us about the war dead, the eternal flame shimmers behind her grizzled hair.

"On these marble steps," she says, "we remember not only brave Soviet people. We remember whole cities devastated in the Great Patriotic War of 1941 to 45: Smolensk, Kiev, Odessa . . . But most of all, the Siege of Leningrad."

In the siege, more than half a million people starved to death. Countless thousands died in air raids. But the city never fell. Others, hundreds of miles inland, suffered similar batterings. They have their own memorials. Russia fought the war on our side, but had more people killed than any other country. Now we call them our enemy. The towns will always be remembered: here are their names. The men will always be remembered: whatever their names.

My mother is dying now. They won't admit it. Doctors and nurses flutter around her, trying to soothe her, pretending they might save her. But she knows. She lies in bed most of the day, too weak to walk around. I have placed her bed so she can look out the window, down into the streets, where she can see life carrying on. We both talk as if she will get better. But she knows. I know she knows.

When Olga moves aside, I remain staring into the eternal flame. I must have stared at it too long, because the bright light makes my eyes water, and when I jerk my head away I find Natalia close beside me. She seems concerned. "It can be moving, yes?"

"Yes."

She rests her hand on my forearm. "Twenty million people —living people. Families, whole villages were destroyed fighting the Nazis. You see here?" She points to an engraved stone, and I blink away this stupid mist from in front of my eyes. "Sebastopol. The whole city was flattened. Ninety-eight per cent destroyed. Unimaginable."

"Yes." My throat is dry. My nose is wet.

"You lost somebody?" she asks.

Without thinking, I place my hand over hers on my arm. "Yes." I try to smile. She puts her other hand on the back of mine, and whispers, "It must never happen again."

Her hand is warm and soft.

"That's right," I say. "It must not happen again."

The tour ends around noon and the sun's shining and I've nowhere to go, so when everybody drifts back inside the hotel I cross the square and go into the old monastery garden.

Sunlight trickles through the leaves of the young trees. It melts over the pathways and seats, and dribbles on to the short grass that you mustn't walk on. In a clearing over there, four women weed a flower-bed, throwing uprooted plants on to a canvas sheet. They have no wheelbarrow. When the pile is high enough, one of the women gathers the corners and drags the thing away.

I sit down, close to a little statue, and sniff the aroma of damp leaves. Everywhere is neat and tidy. Within these walls are hardly any people, and no cars. Everywhere is peaceful, like I say.

I ease myself on the wooden bench, and look around. Over where a track joins this path to another, Natalia scurries between the trees. When she reaches the other path she glances back. Then she turns and slips away.

So what do you think—I nip along the path, touch her arm, and whisk her off for a cuddly afternoon? You're wrong. I stay put. I muse on what she was doing here.

Sure, it is nice to know she's interested. Sure, I could catch her beneath the trees. But when it comes to sweet-talking women, they left me out.

Apart from April. Suddenly, under these drowsy trees, the memory of her comes flooding back. You know how it is. She was not a whisper in your brain, yet in an instant she's as sharp as a reflection in the mirror. All the pain of betrayal, as real as the day it happened.

For two years we were as close as twins. We did everything together—holidays, cars, clothes. Anything that cost money. Then I went inside. Wait for me, April, it won't be long. I could be out in two years eight months, April. That's not long.

But April couldn't wait two years eight months. She couldn't wait the eight months alone. Not her.

So I only had one visitor, for five years. Me and Ma were close-knit. When Dad died we gripped together like ivy on a tree. Times had been hard. We'd had appearances to keep up. We had a reputation—his reputation—for being hard to deal with, bad to cross. We didn't mind. To the little men round our way we looked tough, though across the river we were nothing. Money men could scratch us out with a flourish of their pen.

In two years we lost everything Dad had built up, except the club in New Cross. Then there was the night the front was blown out, and that was the end of that, too. Dad would have known what to do. He'd have hammered back. I was just a kid—impulsive, inexperienced. I took his gun to sort them out, like he'd have done. But I blew my chance: charred the back of the house, hurt nobody. The Richardsons just waited for the cops to arrive.

Ma had to continue on her own. No Dad, no club, no me. No chance. Word got around. And once the word is out you might as well quit struggling. That's what she thought.

Ma quit struggling, and last year she called in the doctor. Cancer, he said, just like that. You wouldn't want me to beat about the bush, Mrs Starr, would you? You always liked to see things as they were.

I see things as they were. The club had folded, I was inside, Dad was long cremated. She had nothing to live for. She was worrying to death. All I want to do is give her something to live for again.

9

Sammy has invited me for a drink.

Leading off one side of the hotel lobby is a flight of steps down to a brightly lit basement calling itself The Nightclub. A glum waiter stops us at the door. "You have ticket?"

We need one to get in. Tickets, he says, are available from the Intourist Bureau. We go back. When we ask the official at the desk for tickets, she says that she is Information and for tickets we go upstairs. We haul up another flight to find the Intourist Bureau. It is shut.

"God help you if you were alcoholic," says Sammy. "You'd no survive."

Gorbachev thinks he is drying out a nation of alcoholics. It won't work. I've seen winos spend three years in Pentonville without a drop passes their lips. First night they are released, they're drunk. Alcoholics can survive a drought better than a cactus in the desert. The more they're parched, the more they can soak up.

We drift back to the lobby. Down in the nightclub, wine is on the tables, the waiter is at the door, but the place is dead. In the lobby behind her counter, Miss Information files her nails.

"There has to be somewhere," Sammy says.

"When you find it, you tell me," I say. "I'm for bed."

I only said it to be rid of him. I could use a drink, but I prefer to take it on my own.

Everywhere is dry. No bars, no off-licences, no wine with the meals. Prohibition in Pittsburgh must have been like this. It was one of Gorbachev's great reforms: cut out the vodka, revitalize the workforce. But a stiff drink is what they need. I know how they feel.

I am prowling round this room like a tiger in his cage. I need that drink. There must be alcohol somewhere. I can't have been looking.

So I ease out of the room again into the silent corridor. I ride down in the creaking lift, stroll across the vestibule, and go out through the glass door.

It has started to rain. A heavy cloud has filled its belly with water from the Baltic, then collapsed on to the town. Soft drizzle wraps itself around the buildings. It soaks the pavements. While I stand under the canopy watching the gutters fill with rainwater, a flash of lightning explodes across the river. Two seconds later, thunder rolls. Under the canopy, the dry patch is shrinking, but until the damp reaches my shoes I stay watching the rain.

Flickers of lightning make the buildings look grey and tired.

Someone is trying to tell me something: be a good boy and stay indoors. Going out at night looking for a drink could get me into bad company. Even when I make polite conversation in daylight, I meet small-time hoodlums . . . They must smell me coming.

I can't let that happen. I can't talk to criminals. I'm a *tourist* for Christ's sake. I've just got to keep my head down, meet Kaplan, pick up the goods. Behave myself, for once.

I leave the moist outside air, and push back through the door into the lobby. People stand inside looking out through the glass, safe and dry. Tourists can watch the summer storm and not get their clothes soiled. Women can wait alone and not feel threatened.

One over there, for instance, wears a smooth suit and high heels and her blonde hair is cropped. She's alone, cool and relaxed, glancing around her. Maybe she's German. She is too assured to be British, too smartly dressed to be American. She's European. Her hair is blonde, her complexion tanned, but she is not Scandinavian. French? French women eat leanly through their teens. Dutch? They are folksy, like their cattle. So I think she is German.

She sees me looking at her.

I glance away. I didn't mean to embarrass her: that isn't why I stared. It was just that she was alone and unconcerned. Back home, someone would approach her. Here she can stand unmolested. Maybe it's the security of a hotel lobby. Maybe it's Russia. It does feel safe here. I thought everybody would scurry around looking over their shoulders. But they don't. They don't have to. They know the authorities are there, keeping an eye on them—looking after them, you might say. "Keep your nose clean and we will look after you. Step out of line and we will know." It's kinda comforting, to know where you stand. Ex-cons fit in here.

Our eyes meet.

I've done it again. Here am I thinking how great it is that she can stand around at night without men propositioning her, and every time she looks up she finds me staring. Typical vulgar tourist. Next thing you know she'll have to move, to get away from the stranger with staring eyes. It would be easier if I left. I'm only killing time.

But I glance across one last time to check if she's still there. And she is. And she smiles.

So with a reassuring shrug to show I mean no harm, I smile back. And she nods.

She is less than five metres away. For two seconds she regards me coolly. Then she strolls nearer the closed *Berioska* store. She peers over the barrier to see what's inside. I gaze at her back. Then, as I knew she would, she turns again, not bothering to glance around this time, but looking straight at me. I haven't moved. Neither has she.

We hold this "Some Enchanted Evening" pose for at least ten seconds, until it is obvious she is not going to budge. She doesn't smile. She doesn't look away.

So I think, why not?

I unstick my shoes from the floor, and amble across. Though I haven't smoked since I was fourteen years old, my hands could use a packet now. I slip my right hand into my trouser pocket, and let my left dangle loose as a mannequin's wrist. I ask if she speaks English.

"A little."

"My name's Mickey."

"I am Galina." She smiles, and waits for me to speak.

"Where are you from?"

"Please?"

"Are you German, or what?"

"I am Russian."

"You look German. Your clothes . . . the way you stand."

"You mean West German, I hope? My clothes are good?"

"Very smart. Where do you get them?"

She docsn't answer at once. Then she tilts her head, smiles, and asks, "Why do you . . . want to know?"

I shrug. "It's not my business. I'm not a cop."

"Cop?"

"Police. I'm not a policeman. That's not why I asked."

"No. You are English."

"That's right."

"You like to come to bed with me?"

I stand with my mouth open. "You like?" she asks again.

I am floundering like the vicar who opened the wrong bedroom door. "I'm sorry, I didn't realize, I thought—"

"You not like? If you not like, there is a bar. We can go there."

"A bar? You can get a drink there?"

"Of course. You like?"

"I like."

Gently she lays her hand on my elbow. She smiles close into my face. "It costs money, you know. You have money with you?"

"Yeah."

"Hard currency."

"I got a lot of roubles."

She pouts. "We like pounds sterling. You have credit card?"

"Do *you* take credit cards?"

"Not I," she laughs. "Drinking bar, it does. I must have money, you know."

"Hard currency?"

"Naturally." She puts her arm through mine and walks me across the lobby, crooning in my ear. "I am good to you, you know? Hot stuff. You like."

"Yeah. How much will it cost?"

"For me or for bar?"

My attention flicks away. "Whichever."

"Please?"

Natalia has appeared from the other side of the lobby. She starts purposefully toward us. Galina carries on: "You like dancing or come to bed? As you like."

I stop walking. "Sorry, Galina, this is my girlfriend."

Galina sees where I'm staring, and switches attention to Natalia. From the expression on Natalia's face, you could believe she was my wife. Galina shrugs. "*Nu, vot, voz'mite,*" she spits. Then she walks off, shaking her head.

"You should not talk to women like that," Natalia declares.

"I won't do it again."

"Only because she is gone now."

"I've had a bad day."

"With women like that, you could have a bad night."

Suddenly, I feel embarrassed. Here I am in a hotel lobby at twilight, caught arm-in-arm with a whore. I look down and mumble. Natalia grins. She punches me playfully in the chest and says, "Don't worry, I won't tell anyone. But I keep my eye on you."

She leads me back across the lobby, striding ahead of me like a female warder. The tight bun in her hair is loosening, but her white blouse is laundry crisp. Her short navy skirt flicks briskly from side to side. Her heels clatter on the shiny floor.

I say, "Western shoes."

She crooks an eyebrow.

"You're wearing decent shoes. Russian shoes have plastic soles. They scuffle on the ground."

"Scuffle? Is not that a kind of fight?"

"No.—Yes and no. It means dragging your feet, rubbing the soles of your shoes on the ground."

"That is shuffle, not scuffle."

"They're not the same."

"What is difference?"

I can't explain. I ask whose language it is anyway. She shrugs. "Where will you go now?" she asks.

"I could use a drink. Are there no bars in this hotel?"

"Shall we try a buffet?"

"Buffet?"

"Sure. Sometimes they have wine."

There are buffets on every floor. But they look like small factory canteens: a few formica-topped tables, cheap hard chairs, a corner counter. I never thought they'd have wine. I remember reading about Russian buffets in one of the tourist guidebooks. Champagne and smoked salmon at the Bolshoi. Sturgeon and caviar, blinis and shaslik, vodka, Russian wines. I perk up.

The one she takes me to is quiet, with two tables occupied. It is self-service. Under a glass cover are some tired-looking cakes, cold fish, black and white bread. On the steel counter, bottles of sulphurous Russian mineral water stand beside murky orange pop. Natalia asks. Today, the woman replies, wine is not available. We can have low alcohol beer. I ask for tea.

The white-coated counterhand inclines her head towards the tea-urn at the end. I take a cup, drop a teabag inside, press the tap on the urn, and fill up with hot water. Natalia has orange pop. On the counter lies a rusty tin-opener. Natalia uses it to prise the top off her bottle. I ask the counterhand for cakes. Natalia smiles, shakes her head, and lifts two pieces on to our plates. We must do it ourselves. The woman behind the counter waits cow-like at her till.

"Anything else?" Natalia asks. I shake my head. I give the woman a five-rouble note, and get a handful of change. We choose a table.

"She works hard," I say.

"Is self-service. You have same thing in the West."

"Back home she'd at least take the top off your bottle. I wouldn't have to make my own tea."

Natalia brushes the loose strand of hair back from her forehead. "Was it so hard to do?"

"We call it service."

"We have no servants in Soviet Union."

"Service, not servants. They're not the same."

"What is difference?"

"More than in shuffle and scuffle." I drink my tea. "I suppose it ain't her job to serve people. She just takes the money."

"You are so spoilt in the West." The strand of hair has fallen down again. She flicks her head. "You pay people to serve you. Is degrading."

I bite into my cake. It tastes of chocolate and almond. Natalia smiles at me: "It tastes nice?" I nod. "And is not expensive," she says, tossing her head again. "How much you did pay?"

"I didn't look."

She tuts. "Sixty-three kopeks. Two cakes, some tea, a lemonade. How much that would cost in England?"

"Depends where you bought it—in a plush hotel or a cheap café. This is a cheap café in a plush hotel, so God knows."

"In Soviet Union, food is same price everywhere."

"Yeah?"

"Sure. Cup of tea is three kopeks, anywhere you drink it. Why should it be different?"

"You buy more than the tea. You buy the place, the environment."

She pulls a hairgrip out from her hair, and tries to capture the piece that has fallen loose. More wisps float free. "Why does your 'plush' place cost more?"

"It costs more to run."

"That is not why." She keeps her hands above her head, fiddling with the hairgrip. "The high price is not for tea. Is to keep people out. To keep poor people out. In Soviet Union we don't have those barriers. No one is prevented by lack of money."

"Are we gonna argue all night?"

"What had you in mind, Mickey?"

She shares a room with Olga. But Olga is out. "She has somewhere else she sleeps in Leningrad."

I glance at their two neatly made beds, the dark plain furniture, the thin curtains. "Looks the same as my room," I say.

"Why should it not?"

Why not indeed. Staff and guests get the same in Russia. No distinctions. "Can I use your phone?"

"Who do you call?"

"My mother in England. I'll pay for the call."

It's about the right time. Back in Deptford it will be eight o'clock. While I place the call, Natalia lays out two cans of imported lager and some biscuits on a plate. It should be a wild party.

When I put the phone down, she asks, "Do you enjoy Leningrad?"

"Enjoy is not the word I'd use."

"You should stay here longer, get to know us. See below the surface."

No thanks, Natalia.

"Things are changing here, you know."

"Under Gorbachev?"

"He opened our eyes. Now we see truth about things."

"Will you let him finish what he's started?"

"We must. He is our hope."

She is so certain. Her eyes have that faraway look, and her lips are moist. She pants softly. In the dimly.lit room a silence falls. We look at each other. I smile. She reaches forward, and I stroke her hand.

The telephone rings. We break apart. As she lifts the receiver, her face stiffens. She still looks prim as she hands me the receiver. We didn't expect I'd get through so fast.

"Mr Starr?" It's the nurse again.

"How's my mother?"

"She's asleep."

"How come you're still there?"

"It wasn't right to leave her. I can if you want me to. Your decision, Mr Starr."

"How do I know? Let me speak to her."

"Your mother's in her bedroom. It would take too long."

"I'll ring back."

"Best not, I suggest."

"Why?"

"She had treatment today, and she's sleeping soundly. I could rouse her, but she'd find it hard to sleep again."

I had forgotten about the treatment. It's Monday today. She's always bad on Monday.

"Don't worry, Mr Starr. Everything is under control. I'll say you called."

I splutter, but she's right not to wake her. When I put the phone down I am in a different mood from when I picked it up.

"Your mother, she is ill?"

Natalia looks concerned, but I am no longer interested in how she looks. She is pretty and it's late and there are just the two of us in her bedroom, but my thoughts have gone elsewhere.

"What is wrong for your mother?"

"She has cancer. You know what that is?"

"Of course. I am sorry. I did not know."

"You couldn't."—Could you? Why are you blushing? What do you know about me?

67

"How bad is she now?"

What's this concern, Natalia? Why am I invited to your room?

"Bad?" I ask.

We sit staring at each other, waiting for replies. But I haven't asked my questions yet. I say, "Cancer is terrible. You just rot away."

Tonight you were in the lobby. This morning in the park, disappearing beneath the trees.

"Is nothing I can say, Mickey, but I am sorry."

In Palace Square yesterday, by the monument. Having an afternoon off. And ain't it a coincidence that Olga sleeps elsewhere? Leaving things clear for you, and your deep brown eyes. You have been watching me.

"You do not want to talk about her. I understand."

The way Natalia looks at me, I could believe she does understand. Her hand reaches out to touch my arm. She is coming close again.

I can't respond to her. My mother is dying. I am stuck a thousand miles away in a darkened bedroom, while she sleeps drugged in hers. We are in separate worlds. Our only contact is by phone, and it isn't enough. I want to walk out of this room, catch a plane home. But it's not possible, as they say here. In Russia you stick to your itinerary. Tomorrow I phone Kaplan. This week we do the deal. On Saturday I fly home. I am employed by a man called Gottfleisch on a job I must see through.

"Sit down and talk to me," says Natalia, but I pull away.

"Is good to talk about it, Mickey."

I shake my head. "I'm better on my own," I say, and I ease out the door.

I think that's right.

10

The streetside coffee stall is not for tourists, but I use it. Under its sagging canvas awning lurks a fat Georgian, wearing a grey sweat-stained teeshirt and khaki trousers. Small tin coffee jugs, ready loaded with filter-funnels, wait on his trestle table. On a blackened hotplate he heats a saucepan of water. While it heats, I wait at his counter with two women. He explains there will be a few minutes' delay, because he has just fetched a fresh drum of cold water from the nearby hotel kitchen. Nothing is laid on out here. One of the women peers into the dark canvas recess to see what else is available. I could have told her. When she asks for a soft drink, he shrugs.

She walks off complaining. The Georgian pours hot water into three of the small funnels, and replaces the pan on the heat. While the coffee drips slowly into the jugs, he watches the woman slouching away up the street. If she wants a soft drink, he suggests to us, she should use the café in the hotel. It is right alongside. The other woman looks up. It is closed, she says, for tea-break.

Our coffees are served in old china cups and saucers. This is the first place I've found outside the hotel that doesn't serve hot drinks in paper cups. The thing about paper cups is they feel cheap, they make the drink taste cheap, but they are not cheap. They only last one time. It's as if Russians thought china cups were too good for them. They use paper ones to show they are not putting on airs.

On the pavement the Georgian has a little boarded-off area with four tables and a dozen battered chairs. Although he has served nobody for at least ten minutes, every seat is taken. People need a rest. The streets are hard.

I lean against an iron upright and sip my coffee. It was worth waiting for. It is strong and grainy, like Turkish coffee, but with a Russian taste. A kind of unsweet Turkish espresso.

The crowds push along the pavements with their daily

shopping. Clutched to their chests are stiff brown paper bags, lumpy with what they've found to buy. In the shop windows are no displays. They aren't needed. If there was something worth displaying, passers-by would demand it. No sooner would you put it in the window, you'd have to take it out again. In this country you don't have to attract customers. They're already waiting.

I stand with my five-kopek piece at a street-phone, and dial Kaplan's number. Out here in the road I'll have to shout above the background noise, in bad Russian. It will feel like I'm on short-wave radio.

"*Allo?*"—a woman's voice.

I have my phrases rehearsed, and I ask for Kaplan. She says he is not there.

I ask when he'll be back. She doesn't know.

I say I have to speak to him. She says he's out.

I ask where he is.

The reply leaves me groping. For simple tourist transactions my Russian holds up well. But there's something about telephones. All you have is the voice, without signals: no facial expressions, no gestures.

I get the gist of it. She doesn't know where Kaplan has gone. She doesn't know when he'll be back. She puts up a screen of generalisations. It may be that she doesn't know, and it may be she ain't telling a stranger on the telephone. But it sounds as if she said he left town.

I tell her to say that Mickey Starr rang.

Certainly, she says. Her voice brightens, as if she might have recognized my name. He'll get in touch with me, she says.

As I saunter down the corridor to my room, two teenagers unwind from the wall. They start walking toward me, as if they had already been doing that before I appeared. I size them up. They are young, loose, and lightly built. One grins and starts talking. They both look awfully decent, like college boys asking how they can help. Except I can't understand a word that they say.

I am on the balls of my feet, as light as a cat. The smaller of the two reaches out his hand. I smack it away. Both boys look reproachful. "*Shto khotute?*" I ask.

They didn't know I'd speak any Russian. The one whose hand I hit looks relieved, but his friend is watching me like I'm a dog who could bite.

"Otkuda vy?"

I reply that I'm English, and what do they want?

He says I'm not English.

I breathe out hard. Swearing wasn't part of my course. In someone else's language it doesn't come naturally. It doesn't flow.

I ask in English what he means I ain't English.

He asks how come if I'm English I don't understand when it's spoken to me.

I now recognize that he is speaking my language, but it sounds like it came from a Dalek whose battery has run down. What it is about is they want to buy my suit. They say they hang around the hotel corridors, and when they spy someone wearing good gear they make a bid.

"You want this suit?"

Sure they do.

This is a cheap casual thing I wear with the sleeves rolled back. The only reason I brought it with me is I might need something formal: this being Russia. Though from what I've seen in the streets the only men wearing suits are pre-moulded party members, and the only suits they wear are thin and grey. They're the sort of suit the janitor wears when he applies for a new job. Trying to look respectable on his subsistence wage.

"I don't want to trade."

They name a price. It's more than I paid new.

"No."

They put the price up.

I am tempted. All I have to do is step inside my room, slip out of my trousers, stand in my underpants with two young boys grinning in my bedroom . . .

"No, thank you." I say.

I push past the boys and continue down the corridor. One calls after me—how about my shoes? I shake my head. Then I stop. I ain't walking up to my very own bedroom door to mark it out while they stand watching. "Beat it," I say, and I wait. They look at me. I look at them. Then they go.

71

They take their time, of course. They swagger away like they were more than a pair of teenagers, like they were men. At the end of the corridor, one of them laughs.

But they go. They are too close to that dragon who keeps the keys, the *dezhurnaya* with her notebook and phone. I wait till they have gone.

They didn't want trouble. It was perfectly safe. All they wanted was what they asked for—a chance to do a deal. They weren't tough. They weren't out to trap me. They were just hustling. That's how it is round here.

When I hear the knock at the bedroom door I am lying in a tub of hot water with just my nose above the surface, like a rhinoceros in the sun. I raise my head. I snort. When whoever it is knocks again, I decide it could be the cleaner come for the monthly sweep-out, so I'd better go and see. I climb out the bath, wrap my hips in this skimpy wet drying-up cloth they call a towel, and paddle across to the door. I open up.

He's a stocky guy—blond, wide shoulders, kipper tie. One of the few ties I've seen round anyone's neck in Leningrad—I mean noticed; been socked in the eye with. This is a tie looks like it's been cut out the centre of one of Sammy the Tartan's cast-off teeshirts. And then painted. It has a barrel of fruit done in all the wrong colours tumbling down the length of it. There are leaves sprawling everywhere. Some of them are green.

"Mr Starr?" he asks. "It is nice to meet." He extends a hand.

"Who are you?"

He looks surprised I should ask. He sucks in a breath, and grows two inches. His eyebrows raise. An enormous grin splits his face, and his blue eyes twinkle beneath his blond shock of hair. His lips are fleshy, and he curves them round his answer. He doesn't say anything that I can hear. He just mouths his name.

"I didn't catch that."

He takes a step further back into the corridor, and mouths the word again—this time with just enough noise coming out for me to hear it. He whispers, "Leonid Kaplan. You telephoned me."

"Oh, Mr Kaplan," I sing out at normal volume. He winces. "Come on in."

72

He flashes another of those cherubic smiles, glances both ways along the corridor, and asks, "You are alone?"

"What d'you think—I always dress this way with friends in?"

"I do not know your customs."

"Come in while I get dressed."

Kaplan stands in the doorway, unsure whether to come inside.

"You got the message?" I ask.

He smiles, a flash of gold like Napoleon's in his teeth. What is it with these guys—is gold the gangsters' badge? "We talk later," he mutters. "Outside the hotel."

Kaplan seems to be taking this hole-in-corner business too far, but I decide to humour him. I whisper back, "Come in while I get ready."

He follows me into the room, crosses to the window, and stands with his back to me, looking out while I dress.

"Is an interesting view," he says.

"Yeah, fantastic." All you can see are the back walls of other blocks in the hotel. I have an inside back room, so I look over the quadrangle, like half the people staying here.

"That one is interesting," he says.

I come over to stand beside him at the window. "Which one?"

He nods down to the block on our left. "Three floors up. About seven windows along."

I find the window he means. Inside, on a chair positioned to catch the sun, a girl sits sipping at an orange-coloured drink. She is naked. She is laughing, and talking to someone hidden inside the room. In her narrow strip of sunlight she is as unselfconscious as I was five minutes ago in my bath. She lolls back with her drink, chattering like a typist on a tea-break. I ask who is with her.

"I have not seen."

"Must be her husband. She is too relaxed."

"Perhaps is another woman."

"You never know."

We watch for another minute, like most men would. Occasionally, she glances out the window, but she never looks up here. Even if she saw us, I don't think she'd move. She doesn't care. It's the first time since I got here I've seen anyone do exactly as they

73

please. Kaplan beams at me, proud of what he found. "Don't say I do not show you interesting things," he says.

"Decadent Western tourists," I say. "We'll lead you astray."

"She may not be tourist." He turns from the window. "We take a walk," he says.

Kaplan takes me down in the goods lift, out on to the street at the far end of the hotel, away from the main entrance. He says he knows his way round the Moskva: he has regular business here. I ask what business, and he rubs his nose.

He draws me to the left, away from the busy frontage, and walks me anti-clockwise round the hotel, where the streets are quiet.

"This hotel," he says suddenly, "is good for vodka, no?"

"It's dry. Nothing but cheap beer."

"Ah." He looks disappointed. "I buy here sometimes. Good *Berioska*."

"It's closed for stocktaking."

"Will open soon."

He brings me round the rear of the hotel, into the metro station on the front corner. Flurries of people bustle out to queue for trolley-buses in the middle of the broad road by the river. They surge past us in the metro entrance, hardly glancing as they pass. For them it is suppertime on another working day. They are going home.

"You have five kopeks?" Kaplan asks me over his shoulder.

I start fumbling through my small coins.

"Allow me."

He approaches a row of ancient change machines bracketed to the wall, and drops in a twenty-kopek coin. Four fives drop out. From the look of these machines, you'd think they rusted up years ago. But they haven't had time to rust. They're too busy. Commuters drop coins in all the time—tens, fifteens, twenties. "Take two," Kaplan says, offering two little five-kopek coins. "One for journey back."

We each slip a coin into a slot at an entry barrier. They are pairs of one-metre pillars that we walk through. As we pass between, I ask Kaplan if they work on trust. There was no gate, no turnstile. Nothing seems to stop us walking through.

"Is a light beam," he says. We step off the concrete on to moving stairs. "If you do not pay, you do not go through. Arms of steel shoot out and catch you. They cut you in half."

"Yeah, yeah."

"You try him."

No thanks. We plunge deep below the city. The walls round the stairway are cream. There are no adverts, no slogans, just plain unadorned cream, flaking.

At the foot of the stairs a woman official sits in her booth. Together with two dozen other travellers, Kaplan and I wait in the brightly lit, red and cream concourse. It is smart, clean, jazzily painted, and is fully walled-in on both sides. We can't see the tracks. They lie the other side of sliding black rubber doors fitted into the walls. When a train pulls in on the other side, all the rubber shutters spring open in the wall. They line up exactly with the doors in the train. We step in. The train doors close. So do those in the wall.

We hammer off up the line in the hermetically safe train. We never saw an electric rail. We never saw the train's outer side. We don't even know what colour it is.

The train is fast. I hold on to a chrome bar and look nonchalantly around. Kaplan is standing some distance away, as if perhaps he is not with me. The carriage is a quarter full. Some people read books. Some gaze at the floor.

It's clinically clean. There are no adverts, no instructions: just wood, glass and steel, hammering through the dark tunnel like a fairground train gone berserk. We don't talk much. We can't.

When we step out the train, Kaplan grins at me. "This is safest place. We can talk here."

I watch the few people moving around us. Most head for the moving staircase. One or two new arrivals ride the other stairs down. No one pays attention to two more men waiting.

"Everything is in order?" he asks me casually.

"I could ask you the same."

"Your parcel is ready. How are you like Leningrad—you have a good time?"

"I keep my head down."

"Is best, yes. Have you changed yet some roubles?"

"Just a few. I used Intourist."

He throws his eyes to the ceiling. "Is no need. Many people give better rate."

"I know. Five for one. Other tourists do it, but I'm staying clean."

He touches my arm. "You see what we must do for hard currency? We give five roubles for one pound. Is not right. A rouble is worth more."

"It's the going rate."

"Because we must have hard currency. This is why you and I will trade in American dollars." He looks at me expectantly. I'm supposed to respond in some way. There's something he wants to discuss. But we have to wait, because another train is thumping in at a hundred decibels. Boom. Rubber doors open. People change place. Buzzer. Doors shut. Bump. Train goes. Whoosh. We let the crowd clear around us.

"About the money," I suggest.

"Yes?" He asks it casually, as if it wasn't important.

"You know the arrangement?"

"Of course. I am not sure if you know."

"I know all right."

There's a Swiss bank account, that's the start of it. A joint account, using two signatures: his and Gottfleisch's. No cheque can be drawn without both of those signatures. After I collect the goods, Kaplan receives a cheque for cash, already signed by Gottfleisch, drawn on that joint account. Now, don't get excited, don't go leaping ahead. I am not carrying this cheque. And I've never seen Gottfleisch's signature. Even when he signed for our meal in the restaurant, he held his hand up shielding the pen. He takes no chances.

In this Swiss bank account are two million sweet dollar-bills, crisp and clean. Kaplan can phone the bank any time to check they are still there. As they have to be. Once deposited, the only way anything comes out is when both parties sign the cheque.

However. Getting currency into Russia is like getting whisky into Iran. It ain't easy. There is no legitimate way. Roubles are a soft currency: they do not exchange. There is no mechanism for moving serious money in, except through official channels, which

76

is beside the point. And you can't smuggle two million crinkly notes in through Customs. You'd as easily stuff a horse inside your suitcase.

Plus who could Gottfleisch trust to carry so much spendable cash out to foreign climes? Not Mickey Starr, that's for sure.

So they use the bank account. But there's another snag. In Russia, Kaplan cannot stroll along to the local branch of his Swiss bank and draw his money out. There are no Swiss banks here. There is nowhere to draw the money from. The only bank is the Novogodny. Is not possible, as they say here.

So here's the trick: neutral territory. Friend Leonid cannot draw the cash in Russia, and he will never be allowed a trip to Switzerland, but he can swing a visit to Belgrade—which does have Swiss banks. Lucky Leonid can draw his loot in dinars. Whether he brings them back to Russia is his affair. Me, I'd head up from Belgrade to the Italian border, and I'd take a one-day excursion to Venice, forget to come back. Having two million dollars quietly earning interest, and with the contacts Kaplan must have, a new passport should not be that hard to acquire. Gottfleisch could offer one as part of the deal. Quite cheaply.

Wait a minute, you're thinking. Where exactly *is* this uncashed cheque that only needs one little signature before delivering two million lovelies to Leonid the Blond? He wonders too. "Do you have cheque, Mikhail?"

"It comes by separate carrier. Didn't Gottfleisch tell you?"

Leonid frowns. "No."

"Strachey brings it. You get it after he's verified authenticity."

"Strachey?"

"Didn't Gottfleisch tell you that either? I'm just the legs. I collect. Strachey delivers—after he's satisfied with what you're selling. He carries the cheque. Gottfleisch doesn't trust either of us to handle both. Too much temptation. But with two of us here, we can keep an eye on each other. Gottfleisch didn't get where he is today by trusting people."

"He does not trust me either. He sends this Strachey."

"You could cheat, I could cheat, Strachey could cheat. So he's put a check on each of us."

"Unless, of course, we work together against him."

77

"Sure. The problem for me and Strachey is that Gottfleisch would then kill the pair of us." I smile at him.

"He would not do that."

"Oh yes he would."

"Where is this Strachey?"

"I've not met him yet."

"I hoped I could trust Comrade Gottfleisch. He said he was honest businessman."

"I thought you Russians believed there was no such thing."

He shrugs. "I do not trade if I do not have cheque. And now I phone Belgrade again to be sure money still is there."

"Don't get the wrong idea about Gottfleisch. A lot of money is at stake here. What he thinks is that if no one trusts anyone, we all know where we stand."

"Is a pity."

"It's a lesson we have to learn."

Out in Nevsky Prospekt, crowds amble up and down. They are walking briskly. There has been another shower, short, sharp, nothing serious. Wet cars pass either side of clanking trolley-buses, shaking off their raindrops like dogs come out the lake. The whole town is awash with showers.

We cross the street and cut off. "Have you done shopping?" Leonid asks.

He leads me into a massive town hall of a building which turns out to be full of little stores like an indoor market; full of people, but not much noise. No one calls their wares, no one plays music, no one laughs. People teem through the shabby aisles, hurrying from queue to queue. The small undecorated shops look like stock-rooms. But the people barge into them, hunt for what they want, and get away.

Leonid leads me into a hall larger than the rest, a room like a small supermarket where most of the lights have fused. Customers prowl through, glaring at the wares. If I was buying, I'd glare too. I peer into a glass-covered counter, piled with smelly smoked fish —dark herring-like remains, tangled up and tipped on to the unrefrigerated slab. They look like blackened seaweed, dredged up above the tideline on the beach.

Behind the counter stands an aproned woman and cans of meat. Leonid asks for a can, and for a small tin of what look like tomatoes. She places both cans on a stool beside her, scribbles on a scrap of paper and hands it to him. She keeps the cans. He grins at me, and turns away. Here is this broad beaming blond cove in a foreign suit and a kipper tie, skipping about like a Norwegian scoutmaster on a dirty weekend, and he's buying canned meat and tomatoes. He queues for bread. A second glum matron puts a loaf aside and hands him another slip of paper.

"One minute, Mikhail," he chortles at me. "Nearly finished now."

I wait like an empty trolley while he chooses a bottle of pop. "What have you bought, Lenny?"

"How do you say—redberry? Is good."

I nod. I could ask him to tell me in Russian, but my Russian is a whole lot worse than his English, and it may be useful if he thinks I don't speak it at all.

He takes his scraps of paper to the cash desk at the far end. Every store has its *kashe*, where you pay the bill. This grocery store has one *kashe* to about six counterhands. So even though you may get served quite quickly at the counters, you have to queue to pay the bill. The cashier doesn't have a till or calculator. She uses a large wooden abacus, flicking the beads as she reads his receipts. This is a superpower? Without electronic tills? But the wooden beads add up the bill in five seconds flat. They're faster than a calculator, simpler to use.

Leonid pays. He treks back round the counters to collect his things. Each assistant takes his receipt, checks that he's paid, and hands over his purchases wrapped in brown paper.

"Some performance," I mutter.

"Is how things are." From his jacket pocket he pulls a plastic carrier. He drops the parcels inside. "We have shortage of carry-bags—just temporary. They cost sixty kopeks." He laughs. He seems embarrassed.

"Listen Lenny," I say, as we squeeze out through the crush into the street, "are you who I think you are? You waste time buying this rubbish, yet you're also setting up a deal worth millions of roubles?"

"Millions of dollars, Mikhail, not roubles. Hard currency. Yes, I do this. I want supper tonight."

Later, when I come out of the corner metro and turn towards my hotel, I find myself face to face with a smiling little portly guy I hoped I would not meet again.

"Comrade Starr," he says. "Is good to meet."

He tilts his head to one side and gives me a "Frankly I'm puzzled" look. "So you are just tourist?" he says.

"That's right."

"But you meet Comrade Kaplan. You do business."

I have that sudden feeling there could be a deep hole about to open in the pavement at my feet, ready to drop me back down into the metro, right on to the live electric rail. Could Tubby know anything about my deal with Kaplan? I hope not.

I return him the same puzzled expression he is using on me. I don't say anything, because I don't know what to say, and I want him to do the talking. Besides, I do not trust my voicebox to speak right. The sides of my throat cling together like a balloon fresh out of the packet, and my lungs feel full of feathers. I try blinking.

"I see you and Kaplan together," Tubby says obligingly. "I knew you here for business. Did I not say so in Kolesova's flat?"

"I don't understand," I mumble. "What are you saying?"

"I say it is to meet Comrade Kaplan that you come to Leningrad. You sell or you buy. Which it is?"

I make to push past him and escape into the hotel. He places his hand flat against my chest and smiles again. There's no force there. He is not preventing me from moving. He is simply saying that I really ought to listen. It could be good for me.

"Comrade Kaplan," he explains to me, "is—ah—wheeler-dealer, yes? Big man, here in Leningrad. My friends and I, we are not so big, maybe. We know that. But anything Kaplan can do for you, we can do also. And we are cheaper. So why you not think about it, while you sleep tonight? I will be here in morning. I am often here. This is—ah—my patch."

He switches on the smile again, and nods his head. Then he stands aside.

11

For the call to come through from England takes nearly an hour. Before then, I have had another wash and am slumped in front of Russian television. When I hear the phone ring, I turn down the volume and prepare to get tough with the nurse.

I ask firmly for Mrs Starr.

"Mickey—is that you?"

"Ma?"

"Why didn't you call me?"

"I did, Ma. I called every day."

"This is Tuesday, Tuesday evening. You left on Saturday." Her voice is weak, her breathing strained. "One phone-call, that's all I ask."

"I kept speaking to the nurse. Every time I phoned, you were asleep."

"What time did you phone—the middle of the night?"

"I'm sorry, Ma. How are you?"

"The Lord comforts me. He gives me strength." She wheezes into the receiver. "Your friend, the fat one, he came round."

"Which friend?"

"He said I should have a full-time nurse—through the night as well."

"Who said this?"

"He got me another one."

"Who did? Who's paying for this?"

"Your friend—Got Fleas."

"Gottfleisch?"

"That's the one. He's taking care of me."

"You be careful of him, Ma. Don't you trust him."

"I trust in the Lord."

"You look after yourself, Ma. You hear me?"

"I'm tired, Mickey. Good night, son."

"Ma?"

Click.

I am relieved she is alive and kicking, but what is Gottfleisch doing in my house? Why is he putting staff in? I pick up the phone.

"Gottfleisch?"

"Mickey, my dear boy, all the way from Russia."

"You've been round to my place."

"Don't be touchy, dear boy. Only trying to help."

"It's a family affair. We don't want anyone pushing in."

"She's very ill, you know."

"We'll manage."

"Ah yes, the Starr family. Independent, and all that. But we don't want anything to happen to her while you're away, do we?"

"I had nurses round already."

"Only in the daytime, Mickey. I was worried about the night."

"Is she getting worse?"

"I didn't quite hear you, dear boy."

"Is she getting worse?"

"No need to shout. She doesn't look well. But if you'd rather she was left alone . . ."

"I can arrange nurses."

"Not from Russia, dear boy. And don't worry about the expense. You're on the payroll now."

"Only for the one job."

He laughs. "We'll discuss it when you get back. Did you contact Kaplan?"

"This evening."

"And Strachey?"

"Tomorrow."

"I'm sure you'll get on together. We mustn't let Kaplan sell us a dud, must we?"

"That's down to Strachey."

"It's down to both of you. I'll give your love to your mother, dear boy. Good of you to call. Bye bye."

I don't sleep well.

12

Next morning after breakfast, as I stroll along the corridor back to my room, I notice a small brown lump on the floor, where the edge of the carpet meets the wall. It could be mud off someone's shoe. It could be a blob of dogshit. But there are no dogs in the hotel, and hardly any in the streets—which are regularly swept anyway. It does look like dogshit, mouldering by the wall. So, because a drop of dogshit on a hotel carpet is something you cannot walk by, I stop. No one else is in the corridor. I bend down. It is a piece of chocolate.

When I look closely, I see there is a two-inch track of dust all the way along the carpet edge, where the vacuum cleaner can't fit snugly against the wall. This is the strip that is never cleaned. I wonder how long the chocolate has lain there.

The thought returns to me five minutes later as I am about to leave my hotel room. When I came in I didn't see the note slipped beneath the door. The door had pushed it against the wall. If I left it there now, would the maid clear it away? Or would she leave it by the skirting like that chocolate?

The note has been folded once. It says. "Meet me after lunch. 2.30. Hotel Kievskaya, room 418." It is signed J. Strachey, and is on Kievskaya notepaper. I try to memorize the name of the street, but at this time of morning it's too much for my furry tongue. I slip the note into my pocket.

So we are both here. Strachey to verify. Strachey to pay. Me in case of trouble. Me to take it home. Simple, really. Strachey and I are on separate tours. He may have been here all week, or he may have just arrived. We come from different starting points, we leave by different exits, we overlap in Leningrad. Neatly planned, Gottfleisch.

Now that I know Strachey is here I find it harder to play tourist. I am not interested in sightseeing. My brain is on standby; otherwise engaged.

I spent two hours with the other schmoes, trailing round a museum full of paintings and icons. I hardly saw them. There was nothing to interest me. I paused by some icons, because they were old, and old things are valuable, but all I thought was that the paint looked thin. A lot had worn off. What was left had stained into the wood: the colour had faded, like on cardboard packets left out in the sun.

Now, back on the forecourt of the hotel, we tumble out of the coaches and say how we enjoyed the trip. The sun is shining, and as I start drifting indoors I notice Tubby ambling towards me. I feel suddenly tired. He is tenacious, like one of those buzzy little flies you can't brush away, and have to swat.

I let him stroll up to me. "Beat it," I tell him. "I am not interested."

"We should not talk here," he says. "Come with me."

"We ain't talking at all. I am not interested in deals."

"Is about Comrade Kaplan. We—ah—find somewhere private." He looks at me, waiting for me to say something.

"Do me a favour," I suggest quietly. "Get your face out of my arse. That way you stay out of the shit."

I guess it's outside his vocabulary, because he nods pleasantly, as if he agrees with me. "Someone will wonder what we speak," he says. "Come. I tell you about your friend Kaplan. Is important for you."

He begins to walk away, gesturing with his head for me to follow him, like he's a waiter who has a horse I should back. I go with him. I have to find out what he knows.

We pass the front of the metro, continue into Aleksander Square, and turn the corner. "This'll do," I say.

"Just here," he urges me, pointing on down the street. He is now ten metres ahead. He stops at the end of the pavement by the next corner. "This is safe," he says, and he waits for me.

I am comfortably bigger than he is, and it's a little after midday, and this is not a deserted part of Leningrad. Traffic passes right beside us. I keep walking.

As I reach him, of course, he turns the corner. I look before I follow, and am not surprised to find Napoleon lounging against the wall a few yards away. Tubby stops beside him. They both wait for me. Where they stand, the street is quiet. We watch each other.

I suppose this is one of those psychological Russian games where each side tries to make the other concede territory. It seems childish. So I shrug and decide maybe I'll walk towards them. Then I realize I haven't any choice. Three ton of Elephant has come up behind my back. He prods me forward.

"Yesterday round at my place," begins Napoleon in his Edward G. Robinson English, "you didn't play straight with me, buddy. You didn't tell the truth."

I twitch an eyebrow.

"You pretended to be tourist. Didn't ya? But you're not."

He raises his short fat finger. It looks like the stub of a dead candle. "Don't play me around, buddy, I could get angry. I know why you met that Kaplan." He makes the name into an expletive. "You came here to trade."

I shrug. There is nothing to be said.

"Listen," he says, and his eyes get narrower. "You a business-man, right? You wanna best deal. Why you don't gimme a chance to make you an offer? What's wrong with that?"

"What is this Kaplan?" I ask. "Some kind of racketeer like you?"

Napoleon frowns. "Racketeer?"

"You know the word."

"Don't try to insult us, buddy. Maybe we're smaller than Kaplan, but I tell you something: any deal he can make, we can do too. He has life easy for too long. Now it's our turn, right? We are hungrier than your friend Kaplan. We make ya better deal."

His eyes fix on me. I can see the hunger that he talks about. I can see the hatred for a stubborn customer who won't listen to sense. I can see exactly what he thinks. Napoleon Kolesova is desperate to rise above the local black market and sink his teeth into inter-national trade. I am his opportunity to climb up.

But I turn away from him, saying, "I am not interested." I try to leave.

Elephant is so big he blocks out the street. When I try to pass him, he grabs hold of my right arm and twists it into a half nelson behind my back. When he has wrenched my arm as far as it will go, he ratchets it one notch further. I gasp. I try to keep the pain from my face.

Napoleon waves his tallow finger at Elephant and tells him to let me alone. He does so. My right arm falls limply to my side, feeling like it has been scalded in hot fat. Napoleon moves in, his oval head inches from my face. I flinch back from the expected headbutt. Napoleon's eyes glare into mine. I wait for him to strike.

But something is wrong with Napoleon's face. While his eyes blaze like a berserk alien confronting Flash Gordon, his mouth smiles at me. His teeth grip together. His lips turn up. He forces himself to smile.

"Comrade Starr, buddy, I am sorry. We apologize. We don't wanna hurt ya. Believe me." He switches eye-contact to Elephant and flicks his head, ordering the man away. "You are not hurt, I think?"

I tell him to get lost, and I turn away. Napoleon's hand grabs the back of my jacket. Elephant waits in my path.

"Hold it," snaps Napoleon. "You oughta listen to me." He may be right. And I have no choice.

I turn back towards him just at the moment the expression on his face reassembles. Just at the moment he dredges back the smile. His cheek muscles tighten to hold it there.

"Don't do business with that Kaplan," he pleads. "Is a dirty rat. Comrade Starr, you gotta believe me—he will pull your plug." I frown. "You understand?"

"You saying he'll cheat me?"

"Sure. I tell you something: he hates all foreigners, you know?"

I grin and shake my head.

"Is true! Is kinda man you cannot trust."

I grin again.

"Yes, Comrade Starr. He inform you to KGB. You watch."

I decide that I have to end this. "You got the wrong idea, my friend. I am not doing a deal with Comrade Kaplan. I am not doing a deal with nobody. And though I am sure that you are a swell kinda guy, I am not doing a deal with you."

He stares at me coldly. "I kill that Kaplan."

86

He says it quietly, and I believe him. An icy stillness has settled round his shoulders like a cloak. He is a true Napoleon.

But then he smiles again, and claps my arm. "We should be friends, you and I." I close my eyes. The arm he just clapped was my right one, the one that Elephant tried to twist off. It still feels like it was broken into two-inch lengths.

I open my eyes, blink away the mist, and step back. Elephant has moved aside. "Goodbye," I say firmly. "We don't need to meet again."

"Remember, don't you trust that Kaplan."

"I'll remember."

Napoleon scrapes his foot moodily on the shabby pavement, trying to think of a last persuasive phrase. He gives up. "We'll be seeing ya," he says. I turn away.

13

By the time I approach the door to Strachey's room, I have
sharpened up. The right arm is improving, feeling now only as if I
had stitches in my biceps. I have had some lunch. The breeze along
Nevsky Prospekt has brought colour to my cheeks. I am ready to
work.

At room 418, I knock at the door.

I have been wondering who this Strachey will be—accountant,
academic or trusted right-hand man. Someone to keep an eye on
Leonid? Or on me?

The doorknob grunts. The door opens.

I have the wrong room. A good-looking blonde regards me
through her spectacles. Her eyes are blue and cold.

"Come in, Mr Starr."

She pulls back the door. I go past her into the room. "You with
Strachey?"

"I *am* Strachey."

I look again. She is about five feet seven, neatly packaged in a
pale blue suit, and she wears her blonde hair pulled back into a
bun. Her jaw is strong, her skin clear, and she is masked by
hornrimmed glasses. Behind those glasses she is not bad at all. She
is also firm about the breast, slim around the waist, and—

"Won't you sit down?"

"Thanks."

I ease into a brown vinyl armchair. A mistake. The springs went
for scrap a year ago. I perch carefully on the edge. She pulls out a
writing chair and sits gracefully on that. Her haunches are now
placed nine inches higher than mine, so she looks down on me like a
schoolmistress at her desk.

"Have you made contact with Kaplan?" she asks.

"Yesterday. He wanted to talk about money."

"Oh?" She thinks about this. Her lips stay pursed, as if she was sucking on a pencil. I am thinking too, about her mouth. The only make-up she wears is on those dark red lips. I look up and our eyes meet.

"So what did you say to him?" she asks.

"I was waiting for you."

"Nobody saw you together?"

As she crosses her legs I catch a whiff of her perfume. I raise my eyes from her perfect knees and say, "I don't think so."

That is less than the whole truth, you may be thinking, but I am not yet ready to play True Confessions with a girl in a Russian hotel room the first time we meet.

No matter what kind of knees she has.

Because I have to tell you that now I have been sitting here long enough to see behind her frozen exterior, I realize she is not just good-looking. She could stun a cat. I wonder if I huffed warm air on her spectacles, would it melt the frost?

"Perhaps we should phone Mr Kaplan," she suggests.

Perhaps we'd better.

By half-past three, Strachey and I are hanging around in the street outside the railway station, waiting for Leonid to show up. You remember I told you how Russians in the street keep themselves to themselves, cast their eyes down and don't look at anyone? Well, they do look at Strachey. The men do.

When I phoned Leonid he was full of jokes. Then he heard I was with Strachey, and his voice cooled. "This Strachey is man to make sure I do not cheat?"

"Half of that is true. Strachey is a woman."

"Man, woman, what is difference?"

From where I stand, Leonid, quite a lot.

He told me to stay out in the square in front of the station. He said they'd be along in a quarter of an hour. *They'd* be along.

"You bringing company? Now who doesn't trust people?"

"Two against two, Mikhail. Is fair, is it not?"

So we wait in the cool afternoon sunshine. We talk a little about the job. We make small-talk about Leningrad. But conversation with Strachey is more difficult than with Leonid. This is a woman with enormous reserve.

Within less than fifteen minutes, he has arrived. He rattles to a halt in a clapped-out yellow Moskvich the size of a fairground dodgem. His grinning great blond head pokes out the tiny window, and he introduces himself to Strachey. "Miss Strachey, I am Kaplan. Most wonderful. I am charmed. Get in, you both. Mikhail, you look good too."

He is alone. Maybe he has decided that this two against two business is unnecessary. He opens the rear door. Strachey stoops and clambers in the back. I squeeze in beside her.

"Kinda small, Lenny," I say, as if I minded.

"But is strong. I wait four years for this car."

"A man of your power and influence?"

He laughs as he screeches away. "You pay no attention to Mikhail, Miss Strachey. He is exaggerated."

The car swings in a wide circle, to lap the square in front of the station and return the way it came. He cuts down a sidestreet, and stops by a guy on the kerb.

"This is Yuri," Leonid explains. "We are afraid he does not speak English."

Yuri doesn't speak anything. He is tall and thin, with lank black hair, and looks the kind of guy who hasn't been happy since he learnt to talk and found it only led to trouble. In the front of the car he kneels on the passenger seat to face us. Leonid keeps talking: "I am sorry, but is necessary you wear these."

Yuri dangles two pairs of dark goggles—black eyepieces on black elastic.

"What's this, Lenny?"

"You must wear. So you do not see where we go."

"I ain't wearing a blindfold."

Strachey touches my arm. "Relax. It makes no difference."

"It does to me."

She takes a pair of goggles and puts them on. "We're in Mr Kaplan's hands, Michael. What does it matter if we can't see?" She grins. "I'm as blind as a bat," she says.

"What is this 'bat'?" asks Leonid.

I reach out for the second pair. "I ain't been called Michael since I was christened. It's Mickey." I put them on. She's right. It is black as soot. I fiddle them round so I can peer out the edge. A rough hand takes hold and twists them back. That was Yuri. The door slams. We move away.

"You can take them off," Leonid says, and I do, carefully. Light bursts into my eyes as if he'd popped a flashbulb. I blink at the floor. When I look up, we are in a beige room under artificial light. The carpet is red, the furniture oatmeal.

Out of her travel-bag, Strachey produces a pair of sunglasses and puts them on. Then she raises her head and smiles into the room. Leonid smiles back. They are two different makes of blond. He is a cherub, smiling and curly-haired. She is a banker with her hair in a bun.

"I am sorry for blindfold," he says. "We make some tea, yes?"

"I'd rather start working," says Strachey. "It may take quite a time."

"As preferred. We go into here."

Like a kindly uncle inviting us in for a treat, he indicates the door to the next room. It is not locked. He surprises me. For a place with a two million stash in it, security seems kinda lax. We follow him inside. I get interested. Here is what I came to fetch. Here is what Gottfleisch will pay two million dollars for.

It stands on an easel, covered by a cloth, in the centre of the room. There are no windows, and the only door is the one we came through. A skylight dominates the ceiling. The floor is linoleum, and from the feel of it, it has been laid on to concrete. We are in a converted garage.

Around the walls are shabby pieces of abandoned furniture —dressers, cupboards, some chairs. At the end of a long black flex stands an electric fire. It is not switched on. Maybe they use it at night, if the temperature drops. This is the kind of room that will cool fast. It will need a fire to keep the right temperature range. Back home, a painting like this would have temperature control, humidity control, crowd and keep-your-fingerprints-off control. Here, there's an electric fire for when the nights cool. At this time of year the temperature won't drop far. Not in the White Nights of summer. Not unless it rains.

I look up at that skylight. It looks new—put in when the place was converted. Out of the frame runs a thin wire. It is tacked across the ceiling, down the wall, back through the door we just came through. A home-made burglar alarm. Open-circuit, by the look of it. Installed recently. After the walls were painted.

Leonid stands at the easel, his hands on the cloth. Strachey has positioned herself six feet in front of it, her sunglasses off. Yuri lounges in the doorframe.

"Lady and gentleman," Leonid croons, "the *Conestabile Madonna* by Raffaello Sanzio." That's the artist's proper name. You and I know him better as Raphael.

There it is. The precious little picture is round—the size of a dinner plate—set inside a richly decorated rectangular border. It is small, exquisite, nearly five hundred years old. A Madonna and Child, one of the earliest that Raphael painted. She is pictured from the waist up, out in the fields, holding a well-fed baby Jesus in the crook of her arm, and a book in her hand. She has a typical Madonna's beauty—serene, dignified, untouchable. The book must be a bible or something, because she concentrates on it. The baby reads it too. I guess he would—it's his book. They must be on holiday, because that is Italy behind them, not Palestine.

The painting is clean, fresh, and has no frame. The intricate border is painted, and the canvas is attached to a simple wooden stretcher. It will be easy to pick up and take away. To me, though, the thing looks less than five hundred years old. I can almost smell the paint. I glance at Strachey. She stands off from it, sucking on her sunglasses, her head cocked over, gazing into the canvas as if it was her favourite programme on TV.

Leonid hovers over the easel like a puppeteer before the show. He may have us dangling. This painting could be as phoney as Pinocchio.

When Strachey speaks, she breaks the silence that has grown without my noticing—the silence of an artist in his studio, adding final touches of white to his highlights. She says, "Yes, it looks correct. I'll need about an hour."

"An hour?" Leonid seems shocked.

"I have a lot to do."

Fair enough. I don't know what Gottfleisch is paying her, but this is the hour she earns the whole of her fee.

She stoops to the floor. In a bag she has various tools of her trade, and for the first ten minutes it is fascinating to watch what she does. She brings out two large prints of the Raphael, and she uses them to check that details agree. She measures Leonid's original and confirms its size. Then she peers at tiny areas of paint through a magnifying glass. She puts her face eye-level to the canvas and squints along its surface. She sniffs at it, as if it was fine old wine. Then she pulls a lamp out of her bag and shines it on the paint. The blue light distorts the colours in the picture, making the surface seem smeared and unfinished. For two whole minutes Strachey silently studies those smears.

Out of her bag she takes a collapsible camera tripod, clips the lamp to it, and arranges the light to shine on to the canvas. She compares the results with what is already written in her little notebook.

"What are you doing?" I ask. I'd like to know.

"Ultra-violet," she replies. "It shows where there has been any restoration or tampering with the surface. New varnish, touching up, things like that."

"What would they look like?"

"Like this." She points at a couple of swirls. "These streaks and patches here." They are the kind you'd find on a half-polished table. Now that the lamp is on, it is like examining the Raphael through a dirty window.

"Someone had a go at it?" I ask.

"The painting is nearly five hundred years old. It will have needed attention from time to time."

I ponder on this. She doesn't seem concerned about that attention. Applied after he had died. "So it's not all his own work?"

While she concentrates on measuring the exact width of a swirl down near the right-hand corner, she frowns. She checks her notebook. She measures again. Her frown lifts.

"No, it's not entirely his own work. At some time, most Old Masters have to be cleaned, revarnished or repaired. They may have been reframed more than once." She chews on her pencil. "When this picture was first painted, whoever bought it would have chosen their own frame." I nod, as if I bought paintings.

"They might choose a traditional style, or one to go with the decor. When the painting was resold, the new owner might have changed its frame again."

"To go with a change in decor?"

"Perhaps. Fashions change."

We watch her for another minute. She says, "Sometimes a new owner might have had a particularly lovely frame he wanted to use, but which didn't fit the picture. If the frame was too big, he'd simply insert a border. But if it was too small, he might trim the painting down to fit."

"Wouldn't that ruin the picture's value?"

She shrugs. "That's the point, he probably paid more for the frame. A picture is just paint, isn't it? Oil, gouache, or in this case, tempera. But the frame will have been painstakingly carved. It could be gilt, gold leaf, decorated with precious stones. A carpenter's gold paint costs more than Raphael's tempera."

"But we're talking about an Old Master."

She adjusts the angle of her lamp. "When Raphael painted this, he wasn't an Old Master. He was just a painter. A teenager, doing a job. An apprentice."

Some apprentice. Some teenager. "So you think he did paint this one? It's OK?"

She stands back from the canvas, opens her eyes wide, then blinks several times. "It looks probable," she says. "Nothing peculiar so far."

Leonid interrupts. "Painting, it is genuine. You will find nothing wrong."

She smiles at him. "I have a job to do. I'm paid to *know* there's nothing wrong."

He grunts. "How long you need?"

"I said about an hour."

He sniffs. "We are here ten minutes already. What else will you do?"

"I've made some general checks. Now I must look at the detail. It will take longer if we're going to stand here talking." She holds her ground, solid as the figurehead on the bow of a ship.

Leonid clumps away from her, patting my arm as he passes by. "We make some tea, I think."

He tells Yuri to keep an eye on her while we two get a change of air. Poor Yuri, Strachey may be gorgeous, but watching her peer at the canvas is like watching new paint dry. He slumps against the wall and turns down his life-support system.

"All anyone seems to drink in this country is tea," I say, as we go back through the door. "Do you have a beer?"

He looks doubtful. "We have some *Zhygupyovskoe*. But . . . I do not suggest. Not for you."

"If it's beer I'll drink it."

"Is very low alcohol. For families, you know."

"What else you got? I thought you people drank vodka all the time?"

"Is no vodka here. Is—how you say—not available sometimes. Comrade Gorbachev does not like."

"So there's only tea or weak beer?"

"Well . . . We have brandy, but is Armenian. Is different."

"I'll drink that."

He sighs, and reaches down into a low cupboard.

"Come on, Lenny, you're making millions of roubles here. You can afford a glass of brandy."

"Millions of dollars, not roubles."

"Dollars, roubles, what's the difference?"

"About five to one, I think."

He hands me a glass of the Armenian brandy. I gulp one back. It is not brandy, but it's drinkable. Maybe they'd spit it out in France, but they'd swallow it in Greece. "Very nice, Lenny. Very welcome."

"You like?"

"Sure." I raise my glass. He looks surprised. For the first time since I took off the blindfold, he produces that choirboy smile he wore yesterday. "I think you will not like it. In England you have good brandy." I look puzzled. "I have tasted. In Soviet Union we do not make so good."

"This is OK. Do I get another?"

He laughs, and this time he pours a big measure. He has one too. "What about Yuri?" I ask quietly.

Leonid shakes his head. "He is working."

We collapse into a couple of armchairs, and I am glad to see that

95

Leonid brings the bottle with him. The brandy may taste like toffee, but it's smooth.

"I better tell you something," I say.

He glances up, and smiles across his glass. The fumes of brandy drift below his nostrils, and he sighs. I tell him about Napoleon, and he does not move. He just sits in his deep armchair, the brandy glass clouding in his hand, and he thinks. Then he shrugs. "We do not worry. They are small-time gangsters."

"Gangsters? That's an old-fashioned word."

"Is not right? They use in movie films, do they not? What is correct word?"

"Villains, I suppose."

"Villains is not modern. Is old word. Shakespeare." He leans forward and pours some more brandy. "These people you meet, they are black market. They do not matter. Anyway, I handle them."

I raise an eyebrow.

"Is no problem." He laughs. "Do not worry, Mikhail. They are little crooks. This Kolesova, what is he look like?"

"A little oily guy, with greasy black hair. Has an American accent when he speaks English."

"But not when he speaks Russian, I hope. I will find him."

"You'll sort him out?"

He spreads his hands apart. "You think I am villain too? I am just businessman, that is all."

"That's what Kolesova calls himself. In Britain, our top villains call themselves businessmen. Must be the modern word for gangsters."

"Businessmen are gangsters? You sound like old-fashioned communist, my friend."

He sits back in his chair, and smiles. Then Strachey calls through from the next room: "How does a girl get a drink around here? I'm thirsty."

I call back to ask if she wants brandy. She asks for tea.

"Yuri!" Leonid shouts. *"Zavari chai."*

Yuri slouches out of the converted garage, looking like he has just woken up from an afternoon doze. *"Chai?"* he repeats. He stares at the brandy bottle standing on the carpet.

"Chai. Chetyre chashki."

He wanders to the kitchen in the back, and we hear him wrench angrily at a tap. He mutters to himself and bangs the crockery. Leonid barks at him to stop. There is a pause. Then we hear a wooden chair scrape on the floor as Yuri sits down.

Leonid carries on from where we left off. "You know why Kolesova thinks he can sell you old jewellery?"

"Tubby got things wrong."

"Tubby!" He chuckles at the name. "What a name is that? No, no, since *perestroika* it is possible to make private enterprise. We can do business."

"What sort of business?"

"With people like you. Coming to buy. Coming to sell."

"What sort of merchandise?"

"Anything hard to find. Everyone knows that when a stone is upturned, all little ants underneath run frantic in all directions. Comrade Gorbachev with his *perestroika*, he has lifted some stones. What does he see? In separate Soviets, little ants run and shout for independence. In farms and factories, little ants run and shout to share profit. In towns, little ants run and shout for private enterprise, for special luxuries. Is good that Gorbachev lifts these stones. He lets daylight shine underneath. He makes things clean and healthy. But when daylight comes, first thing he sees is all those little ants no one saw before, running frantic round and round. Soon they will disappear, become part of new society. Always it happens this way. In America, in 1920s, gangsters ran like ants. Then they hid. It was after a war. Now, in Soviet Union, we are after a war in Afghanistan. Many young men killed. Many more have learnt independence, how to fight for themselves."

"Kolesova was no soldier."

"Not him, no. But young men who came home, trained to fight. They bring their guns."

"Army guns?"

"Of course. You know, *Izvestia* says there are seventeen million guns in Soviet Union not registered to authorities. That is one gun for every sixteen persons. I tell you, Mickey, here is like America in Twenties. Is exciting, yes?"

"*And* you've got Prohibition."

"No." He laughs. "That is temporary adjustment. Comrade Gorbachev, he thinks that because he does not drink, Soviet people copy him. He cannot always be right."

"More likely they'll drive *him* to drink." I raise my glass. "Is there anything to chase this down?"

Leonid yells to Yuri in the kitchen. *"Yuri, gde zhe chai?"*

"Sejchas, prinesu."

Crockery clatters on a tin tray, and Yuri emerges from the doorway. He trudges across the room, makes a point of pausing before the brandy bottle and carefully walking round it, then he places the tray on the floor. Leonid tells him to take a cup into Strachey. He sighs and does so. I pick one up. The tea is served black, in cheap china cups. A fine dust of tea-leaves floats on the surface. But the tea smells sweet and the taste is light and refreshing.

"She takes a long time," Leonid remarks.

"Wants to do a good job."

"Your Mr Gottfleisch, does he trust her?"

"That's why she's here."

"She handles his money?"

"This time."

"Hmm." He puts down his teacup and reaches for the brandy bottle. "More?" I shake my head. But he pours anyway, and hands one across. I leave it untasted, waiting for what he has to say.

"You know, is very famous, this painting. A treasure of Soviet Union. Many countries like to have her. But they know it cannot leave here."

I don't say anything. I let him chew through this on his own. Soon he'll get to the gristle.

"If Soviet Union put Raphael on open market, many countries want to buy. How much you think they pay?"

I shrug.

"Guess, Mikhail. How much they pay?"

"Three million?"

He laughs. He thinks I'm joking. "No, be serious."

What do I know about paintings? "Five million? Ten?"

"This is Madonna of Raphael, Misha. Five hundred years old.

Painting like this never is sold. Our government could get fifty million for her."

"Fifty!" I laugh. "Well, maybe they should, Lenny. It would solve a few problems."

"It would show the West that we have failed. They would say that we must sell state treasures to pay our debts. We can never admit that. Not in Soviet Union."

He glares into his brandy glass. It is empty. I wait.

"What I say to you, Mikhail, is this: I rob my country. You know it is true. I steal a most precious thing, and sell to the West. I am traitor. I hate to do this."

Suddenly he puts his glass down and looks me in the eye. "I think perhaps I cannot sell."

"Really?"

"Really." He sighs. "Madonna is worth so much more money. I have to pay very big expenses."

He wants me to ask what kind of expenses, but I don't. So he tells me anyway.

"To find your Mr Gottfleisch, it was very expensive for me. In Soviet Union, we cannot just hop on a plane, or telephone London."

"I phone easily enough."

"But you are tourist. You phone from hotel. No, to meet Mr Gottfleisch I must go to Belgrade. Is not easy."

"It's your side of the Iron Curtain."

He snorts. "In Soviet Union we need permission to visit another *town*. For flying to Belgrade, was very difficult and very expensive. I must go several times. But that is not all. How do you think I arrange to have Madonna come out of Hermitage and into here? Expensive. How do I have a copy put in its place?"

"A copy? This painting has been copied?"

"Of course. Is most famous painting in Hermitage. Thousands of visitors queue to look at her every day. She cannot just disappear."

"You telling me there are thousands of people this minute staring at a fake?"

"Yes, but is good fake. Those people are tourists. They would not notice if we paint on cardboard. They saw painting in guidebook. Now they see same beautiful painting in Hermitage. What do they know?"

"You must get *some* experts come through there."

"Sure. They stand in crowd for thirty seconds, people bumping them, people in their way. Is same for them: Madonna is in Hermitage where she always is—of course she is genuine. How could she not be? They cannot touch her, examine her, like your Miss Strachey, but they *know* it is Madonna. No one who looks at famous painting, standing where it always stands, expects anything except that she is real thing."

I drain the dregs of my tea. Bits of twig lie in the bottom. Brown tea stains have discoloured the china inside the cup.

"You look surprising," continues Leonid. "But in your Tower of London, your Crown Jewels, they are not real. They are fakes, yes? Real ones, they are stored in bank vault. Everybody pays to see fakes."

"Don't give me that."

"Is true. Your Queen, which jewels did she wear for coronation —real or fake?"

"Real."

"Among all those people? Walking through such crowds—you are sure?"

"How do I know?"

"Precisely."

I smile. "OK Lenny, I believe you. But you're still going ahead with the sale?"

He stops. "Ah. I do not think so. Has cost me so much money. Most of my small profit will disappear."

"You want to up the price?"

He inclines his head.

"It's too late for that, Lenny. The way I see it, you've already invested time and money. To get your money back, you have to sell."

"Ah." He scratches at his cheek. "But it does not have to be to you."

"You won't find another buyer."

"Many people are interested."

"Yeah?"

"Someone has offered more."

"Gottfleisch will not be pleased."

"Is true."

"So why are we here? Why is Strachey checking it over?"

He hesitates. Me, I am relaxed about this. We are horse-trading: he wants a higher price. Eventually he will name a figure, I shall pass it on to Gottfleisch, and both of them can haggle. If they come to an agreement, I carry on. If not, I go home. It's all the same to me. It ain't my money.

Except it *is* my money.

Gottfleisch will not hand over my tiny percentage for nothing. I could end up in London as poor as when I started.

Leonid is talking again: "Perhaps Mr Gottfleisch will pay more, once Miss Strachey confirms painting is genuine."

"You think so?"

"On Madonna he will make enormous profit. Why should he not invest a little more?"

"He knows you need to sell, Leonid."

"But someone has offered more."

"Who?"

He smiles.

"Why should Gottfleisch believe this?"

"If he does not pay more, he will not have my painting."

Your painting, is it now? Well. Maybe you're bluffing. Maybe you're not. Gottfleisch can puzzle that out for himself. We sit looking at each other, till he glances away to the door into the garage. "Your Miss Strachey takes a long time."

"She's meticulous."

He calls in to her: "How much longer, Miss Strachey?"

"Nearly finished."

"Well, Lenny," I say, settling back warily in my armchair. "How much more does he have to pay?"

14

After supper, Strachey and I place the call to Gottfleisch. We will talk to him together: a kind of international business meeting from my bedroom. At the table by the window, Strachey sits, cool and correct in her light grey business suit, her blonde hair still scraped back in its bun. She reads a book through her hornrimmed glasses.

The book is about art. She concentrates on it. Whenever I say anything, she replies in a monosyllable. She is excluding me. She doesn't want to make contact. Not in my bedroom.

I quit, and move into the bathroom to freshen up. In the mirror is that tired-looking guy. He has that prison pallor again, as if he needed fresh air.

I call through to Strachey that I am going to wash my hair, and does she mind? She does not. She doesn't mind what I do.

So I strip off my shirt, run hot water from the shower, and plunge my head underneath. If this latest piece of news will go down badly with Gottfleisch, it goes down even worse with me. I cannot go home and not get paid.

For six years I have earned peanuts. Maybe you think a guy doesn't need money, locked up inside. But jail doesn't wipe out your debts. And ours were rising. Ma earned a little, we had savings. But you'd be surprised how fast they go—like this shampoo in the bath, swirling down the drain. With Dad gone, life was not the same. Me and Ma weren't tough enough, that's the truth of it. We had no answer for the hard men who came to call.

For those two years before I was put away, our reputation stayed high. Our name was Starr. People assumed we were still cock of the heap. Maybe we looked tougher than we were. Maybe people thought leopards don't change their spots.

Maybe it's like Leonid said about the Raphael in the Hermitage. People see you still there where they expect to see you, so they don't question. They know who you are. You can't have changed.

Things could have worked out. We could have come through. Then they smashed the club's front in. Then I went to pay them back.

The phone is ringing.

I shake water from my head, and grab a towel. When I barge out into the bedroom, Strachey already has the receiver in her hand and has started talking. Through her hornrimmed spectacles, she stares at me coldly like this was *her* room, and I was a plumber who arrived late. As she watches me, she continues talking into the mouthpiece. She says, "It's the real thing all right. I spent an hour on it."

I dry my hair some more while she continues. "They left me alone most of the time . . . Absolutely."

I dab at some water which has dripped on to my chest.

"Ultra-violet" . . . she says. "A hypodermic to pull a section. But it won't show anything. It's a transfer, isn't it? Not deep enough."

I chuck the towel on to the bed, and sniff back some water that is tickling my nose.

"Of course he's here—oh, don't be silly." She hands me the phone. Neither of us move. We stay facing each other as I raise it to my ear. I say, "You're not the type to be silly, Gottfleisch. What did you say to the girl?"

"I asked what she was doing in your bedroom, dear boy. Didn't I tell you you'd get on?"

"Kaplan wants more money."

"Yes? How much?"

"Another million."

"A million!"

"He says you have a rival."

"Called?"

"He won't say."

"For that I should pay a million?"

"What do we tell him?"

"Tell him to call me. This is *his* idea, isn't it, Mickey?"

"How do you mean?"

"A million dollars."

"Yeah?"

"Goes a long way."

"Listen Gottfleisch, I could get offended. I have not set up a one-million-dollar scam with some Russian I only just met. I work for you. You have to trust me."

"I trusted *him*. But no offence, dear boy. It's what I expected. I'd better ring friend Kaplan myself."

"He'd prefer that. Do you know how to get hold of him?"

"Who gave you his number?"

"You did. Do we assume the deal is still on?"

"Certainly, for the time being. Give my love to Strachey. Metaphorically, of course." He rings off. I tell Strachey that he sends his love. She shrugs.

"D'you think Gottfleisch will pay?" I ask.

She nods immediately. "Yes, he'll agree. Though he'll haggle."

"But can Gottfleisch get another million into Belgrade by Friday?"

"Belgrade?"

"Kaplan will phone the bank there. He won't part with the picture till the cash is in the account."

"I didn't know you knew about Belgrade. I'm supposed to be handling that."

"You are."

She nods slowly. "Gottfleisch was ready for a hike. He gave me a second cheque."

"A blank cheque—from Gottfleisch?"

"To a maximum of one million five."

"That's a lot of money."

"Yes," she says, in a way that shows she knows why I said it, "but the cheque needs Kaplan's signature."

"One and a half million," I muse.

"*Not exceeding* one and a half. This will be the first time I've written a cheque for a million dollars." She smiles suddenly—a schoolgirl's smile.

"I couldn't write a cheque that big. My hand would get the shakes." I grin. "How much of the three million do you think Kaplan will keep?"

"Three?"

"Three. The original two, plus the one that you write."

She studies me. Through those hornrimmed glasses her cool blue eyes are enormous. She asks, "Why only three million?"

Only three million dollars! I stand with my hair still dripping on to my shoulders. "Two plus one is three, isn't it?"

"The original deal was for four. Add one makes five."

"Four? Four million dollars?"

"Did Gottfleisch tell you it was two?"

I nod.

With her back to the window, she watches me. Then she removes her glasses, starts to say something, and changes her mind. She puts an end of her spectacle frame between her lips and clicks it against her teeth. I wait for her to speak. She points at me with the hornrims. "Are you on commission?"

"Half a per cent." It doesn't sound much. But half a per cent of an extra two million is a lot of dough. Especially when you're cheated out of it.

She laughs softly, and places the spectacles on the low table. "What's ten thousand between friends?"

"A hundred per cent of what I earn."

Someone knocks at the door.

I have a feeling this may be Leonid, so I stroll over and open it wide. It is not Leonid. It is a girl. "Are you dressing?" she asks.

"Natalia," I say suddenly. "Come in."

She has changed out of her usual clothing into a sloppy white sweater and blue jeans. Her dark hair hangs loose. Which is why I didn't recognize her straight away. She is softer and more approachable, like a policewoman after hours.

To come into the room she has to squeeze past me. The touch of her woollen sweater against my skin reminds me that I am not wearing a shirt. Natalia glides past the bathroom door and stops where the corridor widens into the rest of the room.

"Good evening," she says.

"Hallo," replies Strachey.

Natalia glances back at me, uncertain.

"I was just leaving," Strachey says. "I think we have said all that needs to be said."

"Have we?"

"It's getting late."

As she swings past me there is a gleam in her eye.

"Your shirt's on the floor where it fell—if you need it." She turns at the door, smiles, and strides out.

"Who was she?" Natalia asks.

Natalia slips her hand in mine. Her eyes sparkle. Her face is alive with excitement. She skips along the path through the park, smiling at strangers jostling by. All around us, Russians promenade in the White Night. It is nearly midnight, and the sun has dropped to the horizon. Leningrad snoozes in honeyed light. Through the trees we glimpse magnificent baroque architecture lining the park. But the windows are empty. Few lights are on. Nothing moves inside.

What these buildings need is to be exploited. They should all be given over to Italian traders. In one season they'd create a second Venice. They'd fill those empty windows with fabulous merchandise. They'd open cafés and bars. They'd cram the streets with scooters, and cars and smiling crowds.

On the roads now is not a single decent car. Buses are shabby, trams are old, lorries come out of a builder's yard. There's no affluence, no luxury, no gleaming drool-over cars, no fur coats trailing on the ground. Back home, when we walk down the street we jingle coins in our pockets, look for things we can buy. Even things beyond reach. We can touch the rich man's limousine, catch a whiff of fine perfume.

But I suppose the folk here are at least outside, under the trees in the evening cool. They can stroll where they like, go home when they want. And maybe the fact that they don't jingle their coins, don't wonder where to spend them, means they have a form of freedom we don't have back home. They are just out walking, enjoying the air.

Natalia pulls me out of the park, across the road, down a dead sidestreet where we are alone in the quiet. We come into brighter light beside a river. Blue water surges straight and true between broad restraining walls, flowing like a highway through the city. On the opposite bank, buildings glow pink in the last of the evening sun.

Soon we turn away from the water, down another sidestreet, into a courtyard. I hear music. Like the first glimpse of sunshine on a dull day, jazz—American swing music from a bygone era—trickles out into the alley. We stop at a door. Natalia pushes it open and we go inside. Up shoots the volume. The joint is jumping, Comrade.

This dark interior could be Leningrad's version of Aladdin's Cave. The glasses and bottles twinkling in the candlelight are Aladdin's treasures glinting in the dark. On stage, a small jazz combo blows "Running Wild". It is loud and free. We push among the tables till we find two chairs. We sit down.

While the jazz soars, we don't say a thing. We sit listening to breaks, tapping our feet, looking round the room. I recognize this place. I have seen it in the movies. It's the kind of Beat Club that was cool in the Fifties. Candles rammed into wine bottles, melting down the side. Formica tables. Stacking chairs. Small plates of food. The coolest things of all, scattered across tables all around the room, are shallow cups of cappuccino—frothy coffee, from those black and white, rock' n' roll Fifties.

When the quintet pauses, I ask what she'd like. But she tells me to sit and keep her seat, so I let her go.

We have aroused interest. Sharing our table is a friendly dumpling of a girl with red hair. She practises her English on me. How do I like this club? How do I like Soviet Union? How do I like Leningrad girls? I nod and answer politely, taking care over my English as if I was a travelling Linguaphone machine. The jazz combo drifts into a melancholy version of "Sometimes I'm Happy".

At this table it seems everyone has some English, and they are gonna play me every word. It is the kind of conversation where your stuck-on smile shrinks across your face as the minutes creep by. But the music is good. The saxophone bounces riffs off the ceiling and tries to drown out the drums. The clarinet floats in and out like a blackbird, the string-bass booms, and the guitar shimmers like burnished steel.

Natalia brings a bottle of red wine and two plastic cups. She pours from a height, as if filling a trayful of glasses. Bubbles burst on the surface, and she laughs. When we toast each other before the first mouthful, the thin cups bend inwards. They don't clink. But it is wine and I slurp it down. I revive like a houseplant after two weeks' drought.

Natalia has been listening to my stilted conversation, and she takes up where the dumpling left off: how do I *really* like this nightclub—is it as good as in the West? Since I know the answer she wants to hear, I tell her yes, it *is* a good nightclub, the jazz *is* like in the West, and I really love cappuccino. She frowns. "But you don't like this wine?"

I grab her arm to reassure her. I love it all. Everything. Especially the wine. We refill our beakers. She has also brought two plates of food, which is required by the licensing laws so we can be allowed to drink alcohol. There are hunks of dry bread and dubious *hors d'oeuvres*.

I compliment her on her big sloppy white pullover, which I do not tell her reminds me of old Brigitte Bardot movies on late-night TV. A young student says he wants to buy my jacket and how much would I sell for? Natalia is annoyed, saying it is the kind of thing makes foreign visitors laugh at them. Anyway, Russian fashions are just as good: they sell in Paris now. Sometimes. "Since Gorbachev," she says, her eyes shining, "we make big steps forward in style. Is much better now." The Russians admit they made mistakes, she says, repeating her familiar tune, but they can also boast of their successes. No one is truly poor in their country —not like in the West. No one in the Soviet Union lives as desperately as do millions in Western countries. They have seen our slums on television. She is making this point as much to the students as to me.

"It ain't that desperate in the West," I say. "If we really want something, we can work for it. It is not out of reach."

"Is out of reach for poor people. They cannot buy jewels and big cars. Workers do dirty jobs or have no jobs at all. In Soviet Union, no one is out of work."

"Unless they choose to be," agrees the student.

"Such people are worthless," Natalia declares.

I trot out my thoughts about how wealth rubs off on other people, how we can stride the pavement admiring beauty beside us.

"Here we have beauty," interrupts the student. "We can wear

art on our chests." He peels his sweater upwards to reveal the teeshirt underneath. *Pravda* is emblazoned across his front in the familiar typeface of the government newspaper. The letters are superimposed over a red and gold portrait of that heroic worker used on all their posters. The man wears his traditional Lenin cap and has his clenched fist raised high. But below his torso, where the word *Pravda* divides his body, his shirt ends in tatters. His trousers are full of holes, and he walks in bare feet. An old boot lies discarded behind him.

"Is good, yes?" the student roars. His girlfriend giggles. So do some kids standing near. But Natalia stiffens and says nothing. The girlfriend nudges him, and he rolls down his jumper. He doesn't look at Natalia. He makes a point of it. Though he lets his laugh continue, it fades uneasily. It's as if Natalia had a tin badge suddenly lit up on her breast, saying she's a loyal party member: she likes a spot of fun, but it must not go too far.

She looks like an old lady who has taken offence. She is young, pretty, carefully informal in sweater and jeans, but she is as out of place in the jazz cellar as a rich man's daughter on the wrong side of town.

The band is playing "Happy Days Are Here Again". I touch her arm. "Will you dance, Comrade?" I ask with a smile.

Later, we walk by the river wall. The light has dimmed. The brickwork is sombre: no longer touched with pink. Though it is one in the morning, the air feels mild. Natalia chatters now, as if nothing had happened in the club to spoil her treat. We reach a little bridge where lovers and friends stand watching the water. Silently they listen to waves and occasional street sounds. Natalia chatters resolutely on.

We turn away from the opaque river, back through sidestreets. I take hold of her hand and squeeze, but it rests as limply in my palm as an evening paper. "That boy," she says suddenly, reverting to the subject I knew she was brooding on. "Sneering at truth. How dare he do that? Especially now. Under *glasnost* at last we hear truth. We reform society, change things that were wrong."

Between the tall buildings, the air has grown cooler. We quicken our pace. I ask if she believes Russians will ever really change. "They're listless and apathetic," I say. "All they do is shrug."

"They are as—what is your word?—listless as nineteenth-century peasants, you think?"

"Yes."

"Those peasants made Russian Revolution."

"That's different."

"We can make change again."

For the last half-minute, the sound of motorbikes has been drawing closer. I hardly noticed: back in Deptford it's a familiar sound. Now, from behind us, they scream round the corner. I pull Natalia away from the kerbside, into the wall. Six roaring machines crash through the lane, filling it with noise, raising dirt from squealing tyres. Bouncing off the high walls, the din is tremendous. As the riders howl past, they shout and punch the air. The last one hurls a bottle to smash against the far wall. The air throbs. It continues throbbing after they've gone.

Natalia clutches at me, trembling. Because she seems fright-ened, I stroke her dark hair. Then I brush my lips against her cheek. She steps back into the road. Her face is white, but not from terror. She is furious. She spits abuse down the empty street. Filthy hooligans. They should be beaten. Shiftless parasites who would foul their mothers' graves. What impression do they make?

I try to calm her. "We have bikers like that at home. It's quite normal."

"Not here is it normal. Our young people do not do such things. Those were decadents."

"Don't worry about it."

"They insult their country. They should be punished."

We stand in the middle of the lane, an inch of air between our breasts, my hands upon her arms. We stop speaking. We look at each other. Her breathing slows.

Though I have never felt so detached from her, I lean forward and kiss her on the lips. I don't know why. For several seconds she returns my pressure. Her lips part, her tongue quivers, but she backs away. She is blushing. Across her cheeks seeps a hot flush of Kremlin-red fire. She stares at me wide-eyed.

I stare back.

We examine each other: two faces across the border. East meets West. Our curiosity isn't sexual, it's cultural. We are more similar in looks than most foreigners are, and yet beneath our looks, beneath our fair European skin, we are from different worlds.

She studies me in the same way that I study her—like a specimen in a jar. She is interested in what she sees—interested, but nothing more. I think if I asked her, she would come into my bed. We would have sex like any other strangers. We would do the physical things. But I need more than physical things. I shall sleep alone.

And why not? I slept alone for six years. You'll say that it's easy in prison—but what do *you* know? How easy do you think it is? You get lonely. You want to make contact. The only sex is by yourself, under the blanket, or with other men. There's plenty of that. Everybody's doing it, doing it, doing it. Everybody's doing it —why don't you? Nobody will think you're queer. You're just getting it away, putting it somewhere. Somewhere warm.

Yeah, what do you know about it? What do you think you're doing to us while we're inside? You think you're teaching us something? I'll tell you what you teach us.

Nothing.

The guys who teach us are other prisoners. You'll say you know that already—but what have you done about it?

You give us a library. Useless old rubbish chucked out of other places, sent to us instead of being burned. Sticky broken books that smell of cellars.

Half the men in prison can't read.

You give us work to do. Sewing mailbags—we still do that. Sewing underclothes for institutions: mental patients, prisoners, prison warders. Making overalls. Making boxes. Putting things *in* boxes.

You give us a church. Naturally. A big room for the services, a small one for the vestry. That's where we waste time conning the padre. Some guys love that. They tell him they're born again, they've truly repented, they saw Christ walking in their cell. All of that.

I didn't bother.

You give us a kitchen and a dining-hall. Those are the best jobs: you eat better, you work the best scams, you spit in the officers' teapot. You also earn a little more, for what it's worth. Because it ain't worth nothing, in the end. So what, if you come out with an extra ten quid in your pocket? What will that buy in the outside world?

You give us a gymnasium and an exercise yard. That's more like it. If there was anything about us when we were kids, it was that we were "good at games". So we kick a ball around. We do body-building. We get ourselves trim for when we finally come out.

You need to be fit then.

Because on the day you do come out, what do you think happens? I'll tell you. You've been counting down towards this day, but the night before, you can't sleep. You get up, look around your cell, and try to believe that you won't see it again. Ever. You keep looking at the walls, at the pictures you stuck up, at your bunk. And it all looks the same as it always was. Just like it always will be. Waiting for you.

But when you go to breakfast, that's when you realize. That's when you remember what it was like all those other breakfasts—all those times you were ploughing through your cornflakes while that other bastard over there knew this was the day he was leaving. You tried not to look at him. He was getting out.

So when it comes your turn, you know there's a hall full of men trying not to look at you. Some hating your guts, some asking favours: pass this message, see this man, take this note. Find what my wife's doing. Find where she lives. Find *who* my wife's doing. Find my girl. Find your own girl.

That is what has been getting to you, deep down inside. To find your girl, find your friends, find the faces who used to be round you, faces you've not seen since you were put away. What are they doing? Where have they been?

Where were *you*, April? Who were you with?

Bitch.

15

"So you didn't sleep with her?"

"That's twice you've asked me, Strachey. I'm beginning to think you care."

She smiles, to dismiss me. As always, she is cool and self-assured. Her make-up, clothes and accent are immaculate. She looks Bond Street. Today I thought I might see the mask slip, but no. We spent the whole day together, out in the open air, had fun and surprises: unruffled. She is so damn perfect that at one point I thought maybe she wasn't English at all: only a foreigner could be so impeccable. Only a foreigner would have everyone use her surname. Twice I asked her what her first name was, but she pretended not to hear. Now I stick to using "Strachey". It's more formal, which is how she likes it. And it's the way I think of her now.

I'm not used to girls like her.

We are lounging on deck, coming back from the big day-trip to Petrodvorets along the coast. Petrodvorets was one of Peter the Great's summer palaces, thirty-two kilometres west of the Winter Palace in Leningrad. It stands yellow and white, among fountains, green parkland and fine gardens: his own Versailles, perched brilliant and sparkling above the icy sea.

Intourist brought us up by hydrofoil, and we should have returned by coach. But Strachey and I dropped out of the organized tour, and let the bus go without us. For a couple of roubles we could return by pleasure-boat. We are tourists today. It's a day off. Yesterday we vetted the painting, tomorrow we collect it.

Today is the day that nothing happens.

So we took the hydrofoil up there with everyone else, we paraded round the palace and through the grounds, we had a picnic beside one of the hundreds of fountains, we walked some more. Never once did she falter. Like a princess, she was polite but distant.

Ice-cool. In Petrodvorets, where isolating winter snows come early, where the fairy-tale palace juts out into the chill sea, she could have been the Snow Queen.

Remember the story? I do. When I was a kid it was my favourite fairy tale. The cold beautiful Snow Queen bewitches Kay the shepherd boy, then spirits him away. His goody-goody girlfriend Gerda hauls her courage and purity up to the snow kingdom to rescue him back. If I'd been Kay, I'd have stayed in the palace with my lovely queen and her cold treasures. I wouldn't have left them for dull Gerda and a hard working life. Every time Ma told me the story, my dream was to curl up in my beautiful queen's warm arms and snuggle safe from the snow.

Now, in this returning pleasure-boat, the immaculate Strachey leans back in her seat and trails her arm along the side. She wears a pearl white suit, and has a green silk stole warm around her shoulders. She asks when I will tackle Gottfleisch.

"What about?"

She raises an eyebrow.

"My commission?"

She nods. "Perhaps you don't need that extra ten thousand?"

"You know I do."

"If he won't agree to pay it, what will you do?"

"He'll agree."

"But if he doesn't?"

"I'll leave the painting here. I'll say thanks for the free holiday."

She looks over the side, into the water passing by. I say, "Then you wouldn't get paid either, right?"

"Right."

I hardly hear her reply. The word is caught in the breeze. Out across the choppy sea the land rises dark and green. "Why are you doing this, Strachey? You ain't the type."

She raises her eyes from studying the foam, and delivers her reply straight: "Money."

"How much?"

"Less than you."

"You don't look that desperate for money. Not you."

"No?" Her eyes are cool as the sea. But after a couple of seconds, it is her turn to look away, to watch the dark land slithering by.

"Well, I am. Gottfleisch knows I am. It's a dull story, really."

"They're the ones I like best."

So in a matter-of-fact tone as the boat chugs along, she tells me. Her father was a commodity dealer who went down in the '87 crash. In one day his investments were wiped out. In one week he was wiped out himself. He didn't try to kill himself, or do anything dramatic. He did what he'd always done: talked to friends. He crawled around the usual haunts, called on the usual people. Times are hard, the old friends said. By the end of the week his confidence had gone the way of his money. He had nothing to pick up and restart. He had nothing to do. He no longer belonged. It was as if he'd had a non-fatal heart attack. He must approach life carefully and stay at home.

Until then, Strachey had led the easy life of a well-off daughter. She knew little of what her father did. It appeared to be honest and respectable. It brought in money.

She was privately educated, and went on to study art history at the Sorbonne. After that she worked in a Cork Street art gallery. She'd have fitted in well: a high-class girl not concerned about wages. Gottfleisch first met her then. He was well-known around West One. He had her value some paintings.

After the crash, her father sold house, cars and boat. He moved somewhere cheaper, out of town. Strachey stayed in London and shared a rented flat in Kensington. Now, of course, she found she couldn't live on the gallery wages. She needed a real job, and in any case, the dealers' world had lost its appeal. In the gallery, no one thought of paintings as art, only as investment. It didn't matter whether a piece was any good, all that mattered was its potential. Art was another commodity. Strachey had learnt all she wanted to learn about commodity speculation.

She watched what happened in the City after the crash. Some speculators were ruined. Most survived. But among those who simply serviced the speculators instead of speculating themselves, effects were less painful. None of them went down. Some drew in their horns for a while. That was all.

There was a lesson here, she thought: look after the gamblers, but don't gamble yourself.

Then Gottfleisch asked her advice.

Maybe he had kept his eye on her. Maybe David suggested her.

"David?"

For the first time in telling the story, she hesitates. "He ran the art gallery."

I let a pause hang in the cool air, then ask, "Was he your boyfriend?"

"Yes."

"And now?"

She stares at me in that frosty way of hers. She says "No one," very quietly, so I hardly hear it. I have to lip-read.

"I'm sorry," I say, just as quietly. I break off from looking at her, because I think maybe her iceberg is starting to melt, and I'm not sure I want to watch.

I leave her at her hotel and walk down to mine with a thoughtful expression on my face. I hardly glance up as I come in through the lobby. But because there is something about this city which stops me switching off every sensor, I do register them. Out of the corner of my eye are two figures that I recognize. They are sitting in the far corner of the lobby, tucked in by the window near the *Berioska*. It's the kind of corner most people wouldn't glance at as they came through the door. Yet it gives both of them a nice view across the lobby, as well as through the window to the pavement outside. They are sitting there as quietly as day-dreamers in church.

They hope I haven't noticed them.

And as I wait for the lift I do not look at them again. I step inside and press the button, and I don't even watch the doors close. But as I ride up to the fifth floor I know I have to do something. Tubby and the Elephant will not leave me alone. They and little Napoleon still think they are on to something.

They will have to be dealt with.

16

First I book the call to Ma, then I phone Leonid. I tell him that they're still on my tail. He says he'll call me back.

While I wait for my two calls, I look down from the bedroom window, out to where the miniature commuters pop up from the metro to catch their trams home. Underground trains must be arriving every minute: that's how often little crowds surge from the station. They scurry to their tramstops in the middle of the road. Twice a minute another tram lurches round the corner from Nevsky Prospekt and slews to a halt. On they all get. Slam go the doors. Away jolts a tram.

The workers are off to those great concrete pillars of flats on the outskirts of town. They trek out along the Neva river, cross another bridge, trundle through the wasteland to the tower-block villages. They walk across scrubland and wait for the lift. Up to the flat, open the door, get in, sit down, ease out of their shoes.

Parts of London are not so different. Our Tower Hamlets area has a quaint name that means the same thing: villages of towers. Blocks there are as unfriendly as Russian ones. They are dirtier, and half the lifts don't work. They are desolate, vandalized and neglected. None of that is allowed here.

What ours have is they're near somewhere else. In Tower Hamlets, if you look out the windows you get a good view: the river, Tower Bridge, Saint Paul's Cathedral. Come out your front door, walk five minutes, you can be somewhere comfortable and lifesize again. These Soviet tower hamlets are isolated on muddy plains outside the cities. On the map, they look near the town. On the ground, they are nowhere.

"Gottfleisch? What are you doing there?"

"A precaution, dear boy. Your mother wasn't well."

"I want to speak to her."

"You shall. We're just connecting you. She'll come through on the extension."

"How long have you been in my house?"

"Keeping an eye on her, Mickey. Have you heard from Kaplan?"

"What d'you mean 'keeping an eye on her'? You been there long?"

"Minutes, dear boy. Is everything in order? Our friend is happy?"

"He seems OK. I want to know what you're doing in my house. Has something happened?"

"I'm taking care of your mother. Let me be frank with you, Mickey. I'm concerned about this extra million dollars: I thought Russians didn't care about money?"

"They think about it. On the subject of money—"

"You've not made a deal with him, Mickey? You're not taking a cut?"

"I made a deal with *you*, Gottfleisch. Half a per cent. That's twenty-five thousand you owe me now."

"Twenty-five thousand?"

"Half a per cent of five million."

"My dear boy, don't be ridiculous. Do you think that every time the price goes up, so does your fee? Hardly businesslike."

"Twenty-five thousand."

"You're lucky I don't *cut* your money, not increase it."

"Twenty-five thousand."

"We'll talk on Saturday."

"We'll talk now."

"Just bring me the picture, dear boy, and we'll talk about it then."

"I'll want my twenty-five."

The phone clatters, as if someone dropped the extension. Ma's breath is rasping: "Mickey—are you there, son?"

"Yes Ma. I'm here."

"Tell him I want to stay here."

"Ma?"

"Don't let him take me away."

"Gottfleisch!"

"I'm still here, dear boy."

"What the hell are you doing?"

"Just taking care of things. Over there in Russia, you're in no position to do anything, are you?"

I am stamping up and down like a wolf before feeding time. When the phone rings again it is Leonid. He gives me my instructions and I thump down the receiver.

Following his instructions, I shoot out the hotel front door thirty minutes later, carrying a fat decoy envelope. I turn right, hurry a few paces, and turn right again into the metro. I fumble in my pockets for change.

Give them time to get on my tail.

I waste half a minute at the machine, changing ten kopeks. I cross to the automatic barriers, drop five kopeks in a slot, and walk through. I let the stairs carry me down. This is the corner station: Ploschad Aleksandra Nevskogo.

At the foot of the stairs I stroll along the concourse, keeping my eyes fixed ahead, up at the two digital clocks high on the facing wall. I don't turn round.

When the black rubber doors shudder open on my right, I step through them into the train. I take a seat. The buzzer sounds and the doors close. With a jolt, we move away.

This is not the easiest transport system to get myself followed in. With the train sealed off from the platform, with each carriage isolated from the next, I have to plod like a Russian peasant to keep Tubby and Elephant in touch. They are in the carriage behind. Tubby has peered at me through the door. He thinks I didn't notice.

I ride two stops to Nevsky Prospekt station. When I step out the train I pretend to read what is written on my envelope. It gives a reason for not gazing about. I must not make eye-contact. I am not supposed to know they are there.

To be extra helpful, I keep well away from those powerful black rubber shutters, so they won't think I'm gonna jump back on the train at the last moment. Before they have slammed closed, I am loping away toward the stair.

We are well outside the rush hour. Tubby and Elephant must feel as exposed here as a pair of transvestites in the Red Army Choir. Behind me, they will be riding up these fast stairs, keeping their heads down, hoping that I won't turn round.

Normally I wouldn't. I would keep my head down and trudge on. But I have to check they're still there. So I glance round. Aimlessly. Taking in the scenery.

On the bare cream walls are no advertisements. Of the few people riding up, some read their books, some stare ahead. As Elephant does. But he probably can't read. Two steps in front, Tubby tries to hide behind *Izvestia*. Behind them, stepping lightly on to the foot of the stair, is Yuri.

Like a good commuter should, I stare ahead up the stairs. That glance from the corner of my eye took half a second. It was enough.

Yuri. I hadn't expected him. I thought the idea was that I dangled in front of the dynamic duo and led them on. By myself. But Leonid has set his pincers working. They've pushed him too far. Now he's gonna squeeze this pair of boy scouts like cobnuts in a vice.

I rattle off the top of the stair and stroll away into the main street. Out in Leningrad's principal shopping thoroughfare are plenty of strollers, bridging the gap between day and evening. I cross the road and continue to where the Moika Canal cuts across. I turn the corner.

In the open, they'll have plenty of time to pick me up again. They can't miss me. On the pavements are enough people for them to hide behind, but not enough to block their view. The light is clear and grey.

I march steadily away from busy Nevsky, ambling in the cool evening air beside the churning Moika Canal. Down here is quiet but not deserted. It is not lonely. A girl could stroll here swinging her handbag, reasonably safe. I swing my envelope. An extra lure. What is Mickey carrying? He may be about to make a drop.

I must not turn round. Behind is the dwindling hum of traffic. Ahead is laughter floating out from a moored boat. I can't hear their footsteps. But I know they're there. If they could tail me in the metro, they'll find it easy above ground.

That large moored motorboat is half the width of the canal. It bobs up and down on the water at the edge of the pavement. Partygoers are laughing, music is playing, and the smell of grilled beef wafts through the air. I hear bottles clink. I see youngsters in bright clothes. I suck in the atmosphere as I pass. It is a rare moment of Russian fun. They have their guard down. They are enjoying themselves. I want to stop, to call up the gangway, to get invited in. But I walk by, face forward in the dusk.

Tubby and Elephant will walk by too. So will Yuri. A few minutes ago, this must be the way that Lenny came.

Ignore the next turning.

The canalside grows quieter now. God knows what they use these waterside buildings for, but inside, the lights have not been lit. Nobody's in. Out here in the open, sticks of orange cloud ripple across the sky. A browner bank of raincloud follows up above the roofs. A chill rises from the water, and I hunch into my jacket.

The next junction is where I take a left. But I hesitate at the corner to check the sign. In the shadows, less than fifty yards behind, are two men. Yuri I cannot see. Not in one brief glance.

Down this alley I am supposed to walk in the middle of the road. Then Tubby and Elephant will know where I am. As will everybody else. I must act like this is not the end of my journey. Then they will follow me down.

That's the plan. But it's a narrow alley. Either side of me the high walls cut down the light. Tubby and Elephant may think twice before coming in.

I would.

If I do as Lenny said and stay in the middle of the alley, they are sure to see me. But I drift to the side. Near the wall.

I pass each dark doorway without looking to the side. He said it would be one of the first. About twenty yards along. He shouldn't have told me. I shouldn't know. I have to walk by without twitching, without a pause. But my feet are dragging on the concrete. I have to force myself to stare ahead, not to glance into any doors.

It is quiet in here. My ears are like antennae, bolt upright. Behind me, I hear a scuff of someone's heel, as he turns into the alleymouth.

I walk in the shadow by the wall. Out there in the middle I'd feel as naked as a clay pigeon. A long time now these hoods have been at my back. I am sweating. My mouth is dry. I am breathing shallow.

When the shouts come, I nip faster than a snake's tongue into an alcove. The door flinches when I hit it. As I look back, it shudders against my shoulder.

At the mouth of the alley they are silhouetted against the light. Six of Leonid's men crowd Tubby and Elephant against the wall. Yuri comes casually round the corner and strolls down the centre of the alley, a gun the size of a tomahawk hanging by his side. In the throng, Tubby is lost, but Elephant can't be missed. He is hard against the brickwork, staring down at a sea of guns.

From a doorway across the alley appears Leonid, his shock of blond hair translucent in the gloom. He carries no gun. He wears his coat with the collar up. "*Privodite ikh synda*," he says.

Obediently, Tubby starts forward across the alley with his hands held high. Elephant remains pressed against the wall, his hands down. After four paces, Tubby stumbles. He cries out and slips to one knee. All eyes flick towards him. All except the Elephant. Faster than a guardsman salutes a general, he lashes out. When our eyes dart back towards him, he has one man crumpling sideways and another pulled hard into his chest. He holds a pistol to the bobo's head.

"*Ne dvigajtes'!*" he snaps, and they freeze like they are told. "*Voz'mi u nikh pistolety!*" he orders Tubby. If there was more light in this alley, I could see the little man grin. He begins collecting pistols, but Leonid has had enough.

If you pull that trigger, he says to Elephant, we will kill you where you stand. No one moves. Elephant keeps the gun barrel against his captive's head. I hold on to my door jamb. Tubby hesitates and looks to Elephant. Then he moves to the man nearest him and demands his gun. He doesn't get it. With three pistols clutched against his chest already, Tubby dithers. Elephant spits out a warning: he will shoot any man who moves.

Leonid shrugs. You better surrender now, he says: while you're living. "*Otstan'*," Elephant snarls. He flicks his pistol away from his captive's head and fires at Leonid. Not wise. He took his eye off the ball. The second the hostage feels the gun leave his temple, he jabs his heel against Elephant's shin and jack-knifes back like a tip-up truck. As the gun moves, Leonid dives. He hits the concrete. I don't know whether he is hit or not.

Nor does Elephant. He hurls his prisoner aside, and aims again at Leonid on the ground. Through the alley a bang explodes. Elephant reels. He folds against the wall and sees Yuri poised for a second shot. Elephant fires first. He is tottering forward as Yuri drops.

The wounded Elephant crashes through the men around him, stumbles round Yuri, and staggers off up the alley. One man raises his gun. Tubby thumps into his back. The man's knees buckle and the shot goes high. Tubby drops his guns. Someone grabs him.

The other men scrabble on the ground for their pistols. Elephant reaches the end of the alley. He lurches round to fire again, and I press back against my door. Every time a gun fires in this alley is like I'm trapped in a big bass drum. The gong beats twice more.

I take a squint round the doorpost and see that Elephant has made it into the light. He has a shirtfront like he dropped red paint on it, and he runs backwards flailing his arms. He is gaping like a dogfish. His mouth opens, closes, opens. As he stumbles backwards, he hits the low wall and trips over it into the water. He makes a mighty splash.

Leonid sits on the doorstep, slumped against the wall. His upper left arm is black with blood. Tubby has been taken indoors, Yuri has a coat over him, and Elephant floats in the canal. Two men stand looking over the wall at him. No one says anything.

Then one of Lenny's boys comes jogging round the corner with a bottle in his hand. It is half full of vodka. He gives Lenny the first slurp, then drinks himself, then hands it on. The bottle was brought from the party on the boat.

For another minute or so we hang around as if we were lounging in the backyard and didn't really have an injury, a corpse beneath an overcoat, another body in the drink. Then a black van arrives. It blocks the alley mouth. The driver's door opens, and so does one on the other side.

I can smell police in any language. Two slabs in grey coats slouch down the alley and come up to us. They say hallo.

And no one gives a kopecking damn. They all stand around muttering together as if they knew each other. Eventually it sinks in on me that they do.

Two of Lenny's originals drag Tubby out of the tenement, and when I see them nod to the new ones I chill inside. They are colleagues. This whole damn sodality is Soviet police.

Tubby's bruised face looks like he has not been answering questions. They only way he is walking is they hold him up. I watch him being bundled into the van, and then glance down at Leonid. He is unperturbed. Tired but calm. He looks up, smiles weakly, and pats the stone step where he sits. I think I am dreaming. I sit down.

"You did well," he tells me. "I think they would not carry guns."

"These are police, Leonid."

"Sure."

"I thought you'd use your own men."

He exhales, in what might have been a chuckle. It makes him wince. "*Vodki est'?*" he calls, and the bottle comes back. In the bottom is a dribble about the size of an English measure. He offers it me. I shake my head.

He finishes it. The first few drops of rain splatter in the dirt beside us. "What are you mean, my own men?"

"Are you a policeman, Lenny?"

He laughs, coughs, screws his face in pain. The air freshens as the raindrops fall. "No, I am not policeman. You think is better I make gang fight?"

"It's what I expected. I thought you'd beat them up, send them back to Napoleon as a warning."

"Is not our way. This is Soviet Union, Mikhail. A word in the right ear—you know? Your enemies vanish. Is safer than bullets."

"You're friendly with the police?"

He screws the lid on to the empty vodka bottle. "In Soviet Union, every family has policeman—uncle, brother, someone. This is not America, Mikhail. Not gangsterland, bang-bang. We do not need gangs here, we need *blat*—what is your word? —influence. Is who you know. *Ponyal?*"

"Yeah," I say slowly, "I understand."

I feel a long way from home. It makes me shiver. The rain is falling harder, forming dark patches on the pavement. It will be plopping beside the Elephant in the Moika Canal.

17

"I have a bad feeling about this, Strachey."

"Last-minute nerves?"

We are waiting in the square outside Moskva Station. It is the following morning and Leonid is late. I ask if she believes that Leonid will let us take his painting home tomorrow.

"Why shouldn't he? He's being paid."

"This is Russia. You can't steal national treasures here."

"He has."

"Maybe."

"Don't you think it's genuine?"

"Seems unlikely."

"I know my job, Mickey. It's the real thing."

"But will we get it home?"

She checks her watch. "He's quarter of an hour late. Is there anywhere for a coffee?"

"I'll look inside the station. Wait here in case he comes."

"I'm not the kind of girl who stands outside stations."

Which is true enough. We go in together. I say that I expect he'll come now. She says he can wait.

Moskva Station looks like an opera house. It has a sandstone façade, and arched entrances. Inside is clean and busy. Silent throngs are killing time. At the rickety stall we queue for two plastic beakers of thick black coffee. We blow steam off the surface and sip noisily. I gesture at the austere architecture: "One of Stalin's monuments to impress the people."

"Symbols of collective achievement, he'd have said."

"What would you say?"

She snorts. "Architecture for the masses. He was like all emperors: he built grandly to subdue people. Back home, we hang symbols on the walls. Stalin's symbols *were* the walls. When I worked in the gallery, symbols were what we sold. A customer hung one of our expensive paintings on his wall, so everybody would know he was cultured and rich. David said our paintings were walls when they should have been windows."

She blows hard on her coffee. I ask what he meant.

"He was full of crap."

I drink a gulp of coffee. "Why did you split up?"

"He was a bastard."

"Sorry." I drink some more.

"I was *his* symbol, to impress his friends. I was young, well-off, independent, but I chose him, the older man. It does impress people."

"When you realized that, you left him?"

"He left me."

"Young, well-off and beautiful?"

"I wasn't well-off after the crash. Anyway, women were like cars to him. He had to update from time to time, get a new model to ride in." She drains the coffee and pulls a face. "What do they put in this stuff?"

"The dregs too bitter?"

She flashes me a cold glance, then relaxes and smiles. "Now you know how the innocent maid was seduced and betrayed. Hurt once, but never again."

"Heart of steel, eh?"

"Heart of ice. The Snow Queen."

"Ah," I say laughing. "Don't say that!"

She frowns at me, but I don't explain. I take our cups back to the stall, and think: never again, you said it. That makes two of us, Strachey.

"I thought you'd died on us, Lenny."

He spins round. "Ah, there you are both. I apologize. I am sorry to be late."

As we squeeze into his yellow Moskvich, he gabbles nervously. He won't stop talking. He says the car broke down, he had to fetch a guy to fix it, he thought we'd given up waiting at the station.

"Where else would we go, Lenny?"

His left arm is rigid in a sling, so he has to use his right to grip the wheel and change gear. While he drives us out of the square, he twists round in his seat to grin at us.

"Keep an eye on the road, will you?"

He laughs, pulls out into traffic, and accelerates away. He continues jabbering. This is either a reaction to last night or is because today is the day Strachey should have his cheque in her handbag. If I was about to get my hands on a cheque that big, I would jabber too. He could buy half Leningrad for that money.

But I'm relieved we ain't wearing those dark goggles. This time he has not brought Yuri to keep us subdued. Yuri. The last I saw of him was when they threw his body into the back of the van. I fall silent.

Not that Leonid seems concerned.

Back in his converted garage, he stands Strachey in front of the Raphael on its easel, and he roars with laughter at her: "You see! We painting her this morning—what you think?" He waits for her to say something. She doesn't. She stoops to her travel bag.

"I joke," he laughs. "Is same painting as Wednesday."

"Of course," she says coolly. "But I'll check it one more time, if you don't mind. I won't take long."

"How long is that?"

"Twenty minutes. More or less."

He groans, and uses his good right hand to clap my shoulder. "We make some tea, I think."

So we leave her and move back to the other room. As we flop into his comfortable armchairs, he calls, "Hey, Kupina!" I look towards the back kitchenette. Out of it creeps one of those wizened little women in peasant black. "*Chai. Chetyre chashki,*" he orders. "*Da,*" she croaks, and disappears.

"She makes better than Yuri tea," he confides.

"Shame about him last night."

"Sure."

"He saved your life."

"Yes—those fools, hey? Two men could not hold that assassin. I nearly die."

"But Yuri shot him."

"Was good. We have six men. They are two. What a mess-up."

"Yeah. Listen Lenny, I don't like you being this friendly with the police."

"Why not?"

"We're working against them, remember? We're the bad guys. I have to leave here with that picture this morning, take it to my hotel, and keep it in my room overnight. Then tomorrow I got to smuggle it out of the country. And all the time you are buddy-buddy with the cops."

"Do not worry. These men are only—how you say in English?—MVD, People's Militia, you know? Their work is city crime and drunkenness. They do not deal with you. You are foreign visitor. Smuggling is international crime. Such crimes are not for MVD. Instead is Committee for State Security—KGB."

"Is that supposed to cheer me up?"

"MVD is not interest in you. They are my friends."

"You got bent cops in Russia too?"

"Not any more. Comrade Gorbachev replace many thousand."

"But you still got your friends?"

"I have *blat*, yes. MVD will help me against these criminals. This is what they will say: Yuri is killed by big gangster, but before he die he shoot big gangster dead."

I laugh. "A likely story."

"You think? Yes, you are right. Is unbelievable. Is too Russian. Maybe they say that big gangster killed Yuri, so MVD shot big gangster. Yes, is more heroic. I think that is what they say."

"Do you write their script?" He smiles and shakes his head. I ask what will happen to Tubby.

"Tubby?"

"The little fat guy."

"Oh, him. Maybe MVD will shoot him and drop him in water too. Maybe he disappear for ten years. It depends."

"On what?"

Leonid shrugs. He drums his fingers on the padded arm of his chair. I ask, "Can you get the MVD to hold him a day or two, then release him Monday?"

"On Monday?"

"He's not such a bad guy. I quite like him."

Leonid raises both eyebrows, and studies me. "So. You like him. Is your friend?"

"I wouldn't say 'friend'—"

"So why he is follow you? Do you bring him to me?"

"No Lenny, he just is not a bad guy. The big feller was something else, but little Tubby . . . Why ruin his life?"

He purses his lips and inhales. Then he leans forward and pats my knee: "I see what I can do. I will speak to someone. Kupina —*gde zhe chai?*"

She calls something that I don't catch, and starts grumbling in the kitchen. Leonid smiles at me from his armchair. "Our system," he says, "it is harsh but simple. I can work with it. Also, is getting better. We making progress. We do not decay, as in the West."

"Decay?"

"Sure. Your country, like America, is technological brilliant, is fine houses, is fine cars."

"What's wrong with that?"

"All is decaying. Each day in the West, life gets a little worse—is true! Your newspapers say so. Your old people say so. We see everything on television. Here in Soviet Union, life is not like that. Each day in Soviet Union, life gets a little best."

He leans back in his armchair. Then the old *babushka* staggers into the room with tea on an enamel tray. We watch as she stoops carefully, bends her knees, moves one gnarled leg to the side, and stoops some more. Slowly she crouches, leans forward, and tilts the tray down. Black tea slurps from the pot. She lays the tray on the floor. Staying in her squat position, she reaches into a pouch at her waist and brings out a cloth to mop up the spilt tea. Because I don't want to embarrass her, I don't move. Leonid doesn't move either. When she has sopped up the tea, she straightens, making the sound an old bed makes when you move in the night. Slowly, the old woman turns. Even more slowly, she leaves the room.

We stare at the tray without speaking. Then Leonid calls through to the garage, "Are you ready for tea, Miss Strachey?"

"Two minutes," she calls back.

"Oh well," sighs Leonid. "We will have to pour it ourselves."

I pour it. Just as I am about to take Strachey's into her, she appears, wiping her hands on her dress. "I think I've finished," she says with a smile. "Are you boys all right?"

"Lenny has been telling me how much better it is here than in the West."

She takes her cup. "What happened to your arm?"

"Oh, is nothing." He shakes his head.

"He took a shot in it," I say flatly. Leonid glares at me. I continue: "Against tetanus. A dog bit him, apparently."

"Ah . . . yes," says Leonid. "Is White Nights now. We were go out drinking, you know?"

She nods. "You shouldn't drink with dogs."

He smiles uneasily.

"About the money," she says. "Have you phoned the bank?"

"Sure. I phone yesterday. Belgrade, she says Comrade Gottfleisch deposits already another one million dollars."

"So everything's all right?"

"But I need another cheque."

"I'll take care of that."

"Is good."

I put my cup down carefully. This is a million bucks they are chatting about here.

Leonid continues. "I must have cheques for five million, or we cannot do business."

"No problem."

She is as cool as a marble statue. He turns away from her, and talks to me. He must think I have a kind face. "All money is in bank. That is good. I think everything will be all right now."

I ask what he will do with five million American dollars. He says he will live like a Czar. "Remember what I say," he continues. "In the West, things can only get worse. Here they will only improve."

"Very profound," Strachey says. "Can we take the painting away now?"

"First we wrap him for you—like in *Berioska*."

"Give me some paper," she says. "I'll do it."

"*We* will wrap him. Drink your tea. Kupina!"

The old crone hobbles in. Leonid points to the studio. "Don't trouble the old lady," protests Strachey. "It won't take me a minute."

"Is our pleasure," declares Leonid.

Strachey gives way. Leonid stands up. We follow Kupina into the other room where the Raphael is waiting on its easel. From the far corner of the room, Kupina fetches a large roll of stiff brown paper. She lays it on the floor, and barks at us to each stand on a curling corner. Since there are only three of us, she rests Strachey's bag on the fourth corner. Then, with us rooted to our spots, she approaches the easel.

"Shouldn't we help?" whispers Strachey.

Leonid shakes his head. This would have been a whole lot easier with Yuri instead of the old crone. Then I remember again. I bite my lip.

The woman in black places her speckled hands on the edges of the small priceless canvas, and she lifts it up. The easel shakes. She backs two timorous paces. It stops shaking. To turn round while holding the picture in her hands, the old woman has to make a series of little steps. She moves like a doll in clogs. When she has completed the manoeuvre, she totters toward the edge of the brown paper sheet where we wait, she arranges her feet, and begins to crouch. We hold our breath.

As she creaks lower towards the paper, the picture in her hands tilts like the tea-tray did, until one edge touches the floor. The remaining edge she drops the last few inches. She slides the precious Raphael to the centre of the sheet.

She stands up.

Without a word, she turns and shuffles back to the corner of the room. She fetches several sheets of grey tissue paper, and brings them to lay over the picture on the floor. On bony knees she kneels beside it. When she has finished, she pushes herself painfully back up.

No one speaks. I look at Strachey. She smiles and shakes her head. I look at Leonid. He smiles and nods his head. Then, while I watch him, a single swollen tear oozes from his eye and trickles down his cheek. He gazes at Kupina. I think she may be his mother.

Whoever she is, she lifts off the travel bag from the corner of the paper, then tells Strachey to step back. Two corners are released at one end. The old trot bends down, folds that end in on itself, and presses down. Then she gestures crossly for us men to shift. We step back. She comes round, lowers herself to her knees, and folds our end tight as well. Remaining on her knees, she clumps round to the side and brings that edge to the centre. Silently, we watch her inch round the parcel on her knees till she reaches the final side. When she arrives, she scrapes up the last edge of unfolded paper and brings it in to meet the previous one in the centre. Where they meet, she double folds so they stay locked together. Then she takes two deep breaths, pushes hard with her hands on the floor, and slowly stands up. "*Pozhalsta*," she says.

I lean down and prod the parcel. It is firm and rigid, without sellotape or string. "*Spasibo*," I say.

Strachey opens her travel bag. Leonid moves two paces closer, eyes glinting. From the bag, she removes a slim envelope and hands it to him. He tears it open, takes out two cheques, and reads them carefully.

I stand unheeded, like a gigolo in the boutique when his mistress pays the bill.

18

Leonid drops us at Moskva Station and we separate, each for our own hotel. I stroll down to the dull end of Nevsky, swinging my *Berioska* carrier bag. Inside is a brown paper parcel worth more than any building in this street. Worth more than any *block* on this street. From the look of these bare windows, it is worth more than *every* block on the street.

The bag attracts attention. There is always one. "You like to change some money with me?" I shake my head. "I give you four for one."

"You have camera?"

I keep walking. He bobs along beside me, as if we were two friends chatting as we stroll. He seems pleasant enough: the sort of guy sells insurance back home. He drifts away.

I wander into the Moskva Hotel, flash my card, and carry my five-million-dollar keepsake across the lobby. The ground floor smells of turnips. I ride the lift to the fifth floor, and pad down the long crescent-shaped corridor, dimly lit. On the way, I glance down at the edge of the carpet, to the line of dirt where the vacuum cleaner does not reach. The brown chocolate slab lies there still. It hasn't moved. Neither vacuum cleaner nor mouse has found it. At the *dezhurnaya*'s desk I collect my key. I continue to my bedroom.

In my room the only way I know that the maid has been is because the bed has been done. There is no lingering smell of furniture polish, no disinfectant in the bathroom, no sign that anything has been dusted. It has one advantage: if someone had been in, I would see their fingerprints in the dust.

I open the closet and fetch out the soft fold-over bag in which I carry my suit. I unzip the bag, lay it on the floor, and reach down inside for the plastic tag. When I pull on it, I hear the sound of Velcro tearing. It is where the false inner lining peels away from the outer skin to an inch below the fold.

That outer skin I have lined with thin foam, to disguise the shape of anything hidden inside. When I rest the package in there, it is lightly gripped by the foam sheeting. This will be Madonna's hiding-place till I get her back home. I press home the inner lining and zip the bag. Then I grab the handle and stand up, weighing the bag in my hand. It is out of balance. I can tell it has something inside. So I lay it on the bed, unzip, fetch my suit from the closet, and hang that inside. Now when I carry the bag it feels OK. It is soft, flexible. Nothing could be hidden in there. It's too floppy. That's what they'll think.

My bag works on the old principle of the magician's cabinet, made to look either too small or the wrong shape to hide things. Elsewhere on stage you see places that *are* big enough, that *are* the right shape. But nothing is in them. They are decoys. When the magician saws the lady in half, he cuts right through the trunk. But where is she—screwed up in one of the two halves? She can't be. Her head sticks out of one piece, and her legs out the other. Her body, of course, is slumped underneath the trunk, to lie inside the table. But surely the table is too thin? She couldn't squeeze in there. Could she?

She could. Especially when the magician has painted what appears to be the corners and top edge of the table two inches down the true front plane, so that the table appears shallower than it really is: too shallow to accommodate the lady. No one looks at the table anyway. Isn't the lady in the trunk?

I use a similar illusion here. When I leave, I shall carry a sturdy suitcase, just right for a false compartment. But it will be as sound as a judge's wigbox. And I shall carry a squashy bendable suit-bag that couldn't hide a carton of cigarettes. I shall carry it with me all the time.

Satisfied that the painting is now well concealed, I leave my suit folded inside the bag, and hang the whole thing back on the closet rail. That's that. The job is nearly over now. This time tomorrow I will be flying home. I can relax, eat some lunch, then do the Hermitage. Everything is under control.

You may think you have seen some big museums, but this is Russia. If you took all the hermits that ever freaked out in their solitude since time and religion began, and if you collected every smelly one of them in their cassocks and chains, and if you let them bring their hard beds and chamberpots, and if you pushed every single one of them into the Hermitage, you would lose them. It would swallow them up. This Russian palace runs the length of a street. Its frontage is avocado green and white. Its rear looks onto the river. Inside, there are over four hundred halls—Czarist extravaganzas. And in those halls your hermits would be lost spiritually, because this place is opulent, spelt with a capital O and an inch of gold paint. It never was a hermitage. It was the Winter Palace, built by Russians at the tip of their empire to impress the world. They don't change.

So forget about hermits. Think of czars and emperors and fabulous wealth. It is all still here. Because come the revolution, they couldn't disperse jewels among the peasants. They could only open the palaces as museums.

There are rooms in the Winter Palace that are painted with gold. And I mean *gold*, not gold paint. The white ballroom jingles with chandeliers, like Cinderella's dreams come true. From the staterooms are views across the wide blue Neva on to pretty buildings bathed in the sun.

Yet to enter we do not use the front door. No one does. Front doors are for toffs. Here in the Workers' State everybody uses the Tradesmen's Entrance. Leningrad is full of wonderful buildings with enormous doors and wide staircases, but nobody uses them. We creep into the Hermitage through a small plain door, and shuffle with the crowds down a long dim corridor. I guess they think that since it rains twelve months out of twelve here, this is as good a place as any to wipe the mud off from the street.

Natalia has not come with us. We are to follow Olga as she presses through the throng with her arm raised high. She carries a yellow glove to mark her out from the dozens of other guides. Each carries her own identifier: blue scarf, red book, green hat, magazine, umbrella, stick.

But I let Olga melt into the crowd. I didn't come for a guided tour.

"I thought this was a poor country, Strachey. Look at this wealth. They ought to sell some."

"That's why we're here." She wears her pale blue suit. Her hornrims are pushed up on to her hair.

"Officially, I mean. Paintings are three high on every wall. If they took a row out all the way round, who'd care?"

"They'd have to repaint the wall," she says. "There's the Raphael."

I blink. Because she's right. It's there. Back in place again. There on its own wooden display screen, stuck out into the hall among the crowd, stands our Madonna with her Child. The same painting. Here it is now, up on a screen, and it's so goddamn close to people, they could touch it. I hold my breath.

"Let's take a look," suggests Strachey.

She inches forward with the crowd till she comes up close. I tag behind. When we reach the front I examine the security system. Barely a yard away from the screen, a length of tape is strung waist-high, holding us just out of arm's reach. That's it. There's nothing else. No alarm system that I can see. No protective glass screen. Just tape.

I guess that if you wrenched Madonna from her panel, a bell would ring. I assume it would. But if you chucked something at the canvas—hell, if you dipped under the tape and wiped your hands on it—what could stop you? Nothing. Not till it was too late. Yet this is a national treasure. Unguarded. Three feet away from riff-raff. It is asking for trouble. Not everybody is responsible and well-behaved.

I glance at Strachey as she examines the familiar painting. She smiles back at me, eyes twinkling through her big student spectacles. Then she pushes the glasses back up on her hair. "Let's go," she says. "I've seen enough of it."

"I bet."

We move to a patch of floor not occupied by tour parties, and glance nonchalantly round the walls. "Well?" I ask.

"Well what?"

"Come on."

She shushes me, still smiling. "It's not the real one."

"You're certain?"

"Who could be more? The real one has a little scratch made by a hypodermic down about eight o'clock on the painted frame. I put it there."

"How exactly do you know," I begin, wondering how to put this delicately, "that the one you scratched two days ago was the original, and that this one is the fake? They both look the same to me."

"They wouldn't if you saw them under ultra-violet light. And their pigments are not the same under a microscope."

"Microscope?"

"That's what the hypodermic was for—to take a tiny section. I checked the particles under the microscope. Particle shapes vary according to the age of the paint. Our Raphael does have traces of sixteenth-century pigment."

"Traces?"

"It's had a lot of restoration. Inevitably."

I glance around us at the torpid crowds of visitors. Some stare vacantly at the walls, some strain to hear their tour-guides, some read books. "You're sure that if you examined this one here, it wouldn't seem original too?"

She shrugs. "It's a fake. These sightseers expect the original, so that's what they see. Come look at this."

She leads me beyond what everybody except us thinks is a Raphael, to another masterpiece mounted on a screen. As Strachey would say, I know it's a masterpiece because it is mounted on its own panel. This one is a different Madonna, indoors this time, with a hulking great baby sucking on her breast and leering out the picture. The painting is square, not round like the Raphael, and has a thundering great gold frame round it that must have taken a lifetime to carve.

"I'll take this one," I say. "She's better looking."

The Mary is as pure as she ought to be, but gorgeous, her virginal boob sticking out through a slit in her gown so full of milk it is like a thousand lira scoop of banana ice cream.

"The *Madonna Litta*, by Leonardo da Vinci," murmurs Strachey. "In the same medium as the Raphael. Tell me, do you think *this* is a genuine masterpiece?"

"How do I know? It's very clean for an Old Master. But I like it."

"Then for you it is a genuine work of art. When you leave this room, all you will take with you is that image in your memory."

"But is it original or fake?"

"Does it matter?"

"Sure."

"Why?"

Of course it matters, even if I can't explain why. Strachey must understand that. She's the goddamn art expert, for Christ's sake.

I follow her through gigantic halls. "Leonardo da Vinci is dead," she says, as if I didn't know it. "He painted that Madonna about five hundred years ago. What does it matter if we see his painting or a copy?"

"It matters to me. If that's an original, then he made it. It's his handiwork, and it hasn't changed for five hundred years." I am trailing through these rooms, hardly looking at what is on the walls.

"I could show you stones on the beach that haven't changed for five *million* years," she says. "So what?"

"Don't talk to me about stones. That picture was by Leonardo da Vinci. It was his paint on his canvas."

"It is not his paint. It is not his canvas."

We are climbing some stairs. "What are you saying—it's another fake?"

"Not a fake, nor a copy. Like most Leonardos, it has been constantly restored. Do you know what that means? It means touched up, painted over, re-done. Paint doesn't last five hundred years. From the day it is applied, it is eaten away by pollution and atmospheric poisons. All paint cracks and fades, just like the paint on your front door. Leonardo's are among the worst of all. He was an experimenter, and he experimented with paint. He mixed his pigments with oils and essences, with egg-whites, even with his own urine. He'd try anything, to see what would happen. His experiments failed. Think back to his *Madonna Litta*. How beautiful she was, how clean."

"People breathing on her all the time."

"Exactly. Some Leonardos are one hundred per cent replacement paint. On some of them, not a scrap of his paint remains. You could scrape down to the bare canvas, and find only the restorers' touching up, all the way down. Millions flock to see those paintings. Does that make them original?"

I look at the stuff on these walls. They don't look so hot now. "What about this Raphael of ours? That's five hundred years old too."

"Nearly. He is supposed to have painted it around 1501."

"Supposed to?"

"We can't be certain. We weren't there. Raphael was an eighteen-year-old student, remember, one of several. Some people have said that his teacher, Perugino, painted it. It *is* very similar to Perugino's Umbrian Madonnas. This one moved around the Diamante family for over three hundred and fifty years. Obviously, no one can be sure where it was when. In 1870 it moved to Russia. The Empress Maria kept it around the palace until she died. It came into the Hermitage collection in 1881. After all that, can we be sure that the painting which finally arrived here is the one that Raphael made in the first place?"

"Is it?"

"Probably. But of course, *our* painting dates only from the Empress Maria."

I look to see what she means by this. She is teasing me, I know that. But I am an ignoramus and she is on her subject. Why shouldn't she show off a little? We look through a window across a courtyard. The lawn could use a mowing, but across the paved paths the flower-beds are full of colour. "Notice anything about this garden?" she asks.

"Nothing special. It's a garden."

"It's a trick. It shouldn't be there. We've come upstairs."

She is right. There was a garden like this downstairs—at ground level, where it ought to be. This looks like any old courtyard, except it is upstairs on a flat roof. Reality shifts in here. "What did you mean that the Raphael dates only from Empress Maria?"

"They had it transferred."

"And what does that mean?" I am growing tired of having to ask dumb questions, like I was some sort of cretin.

"Raphael painted the original on to a wooden panel, but

140

eventually, after nearly four hundred years, his wood split and rotted. So in the last century the painting was very carefully removed from the old wood on to canvas."

"You're kidding. They can't do that."

"They can. In the 1880s the Hermitage was a centre of excellence for transfer. Leonardo's *Madonna Litta* that you saw downstairs was transferred in the same way. So was his *Benois Madonna*, and Giorgione's, and—"

"I believe you."

She grins. "So what does it mean if I tell Gottfleisch that his Raphael is an original? This isn't the kind of untouched painting where I can peel back the layers of history. I can't check below the encrusted paint to find the typical Italian light ground beneath. I can't examine the physical surface—the wood Raphael painted on. I won't find gypsum-based gesso or characteristic charcoal underdrawing. All I will find is a sheet of nineteenth-century canvas and progressively modern paint."

I feel I am wasting my time here. "So we don't have an original after all?"

"Of course we do. If we experts say that this constitutes an original, than that is what it is. The word 'original' means what we say it does. I'm just defining my terms."

A woman is having trouble with her kid. He is about eight years old. She wants to haul round the whole of the Hermitage, to see everything there is to see. He's had enough. When he tries to sit in one of the wide window-seats, a *babushka* moves him on. Windowseats are not for sitting in. Some of the halls have chairs. He should use those. The mother mutters in the boy's ear. She tells him to behave. He stares back at her, too tired to argue. Eventually, he lets her drag him on. He has his thumb in his mouth, and he looks at the walls with an expression of hate. He won't care if he doesn't see another painting the whole of his life. Art sucks.

Through gloomy galleries we continue past dark European canvases, gradually coming closer to the light and colour of Impressionists on the top floors.

"Look at these Dutch masters." She indicates an army of

brooding brown portraits on the high walls. They are as interesting as a row of filing cabinets.

"Could do with a clean," I say.

"They are labelled as Rembrandts," she says. "But is that what they are?"

"Is that a serious question?"

"Back in the Twenties, all the known Rembrandts were carefully listed in definitive catalogues. Since then we've had a rethink. Half have been demoted. We now say they are not Rembrandts after all. We don't know that—we're just uncertain about them. But they are the same pictures, so what has changed? Only the label. Change the label, slash the price."

"I got clothes like that."

"All that has happened is that the new art critics disagree with the old. The young always denigrate the old. It's how we make our mark."

In a vast hall that drips with gold we tag behind another British tour. The guide points to the gilded ceilings. "In Great Patriotic War, Nazi bombers destroyed part of this roof. Rain came in. It ruined decoration, and damaged much gold leaf. Rainwater simply washed it away. But Soviet workers repaired everything, and replaced all gold leaf like new."

"In wartime?" someone queries.

"We had to work immediately, to stop rain coming in. It caused great damage."

"Did they replace the gold leaf then—in wartime?"

"Of course. We do not let enemies destroy our treasures. Before war ended, all of this was restored. Now, if I did not tell you, you would not know. Is good, yes?"

Outside, millions were starving. Soldiers were without ammunition. The economy was crippled, and never recovered. But when a national treasure was damaged, money and workers were immediately poured in. Every detail of the costly gold leaf was carefully restored. Appearances had to be maintained.

At the top of the Hermitage are the Impressionist galleries. "And the Post-Impressionists," Strachey says. Picasso, Pissarro, Manet and Monet, Degas, Derain, Cézanne and Gauguin. She recites the names.

Here, daylight blazes in. Large modern windows allow the northern sun to flood through and drown the rooms with light. Singing from the walls are bright, vibrant pictures. On a wall to itself hangs a Matisse the size of a truck, in which huge melon-hipped women dance in a ring. There are paintings here you could pick up and hug.

"Are these fakes too?" I ask her.

"Do they look fake?"

"They look great."

"Then they're not fakes. Even if they are not originals, they are alive for you."

"The truth, Strachey."

"They're all genuine. These Impressionists were bought in the last century by Russian merchants travelling in France, and were seized after the Revolution. But when they were bought, the artists weren't famous. They were making their names. Since that Revolution the Russians have bought nothing. So they haven't been in the market for fakes. What we see here should be clean untouched originals—provided Leonid hasn't sold any off!"

We leave the Winter Palace as we first went in: through dusty basement corridors littered with old chairs and planks of wood. Maybe the idea is to reacclimatize us to the bleakness outside, like being passed through the vacuum chamber of a submarine. But in the fresh air outside the Winter Palace we emerge into old Russia: one of those enormous squares they do so well. Around us, crowds meander, horse-drawn buggies trot past, the chrome on a dozen tourist buses glints in the summer sunshine.

It's a pleasure to be outside. But I don't want to leave my suitbag alone for too long. We rejoin the rest of the tour party to catch the free bus back to my hotel. Once we're seated, I tell Strachey that I am worried about Leonid. She asks why.

I lean across to whisper in her ear. "I don't trust him. He is too close to the authorities. It makes me nervous. I think I may not be allowed to take this painting out."

Strachey glances round to check there's no one in the seat behind us. "You think Customs will stop you?"

"Yeah, what a coincidence that would be. Leonid has handed over the picture, has fulfilled his part of the bargain and been paid. Is it his fault if I am caught in a random check?"

"You'll get the painting through. You're meant to. But don't stir things up with Leonid. The less agitated he becomes, the better. Let him go to bed and nurse his injured arm."

"What do you mean, 'I'm *meant* to'?"

Strachey doesn't reply straight away. Obviously, there's more to tell me. But, around us, the bus is filling up. Suddenly she clutches the sleeve of my jacket and says, "I have to talk to you—but somewhere private. Can we go to your room?"

"Anytime, Strachey."

But if I'm expecting a seduction scene in my bedroom, I am disappointed. She is totally businesslike. In a quiet, level tone, she tells me her secret. "Leonid believes the painting he sold us is a fake. He *wants* us to take it home."

"He thinks our one is a fake? And the one in the Hermitage is the original?"

"No, he knows that one's just for tourists. I think he has several copies."

"What are you saying—none of them are original? Everything is fake?"

"I don't like the word 'original'. One of them is *authentic*: the nineteenth-century transfer of Raphael's work."

"Which one is that?"

"It's the one we bought."

I am slipping back into the world of the unreal. And because I don't follow what is happening here, I ask her to explain.

"Back in that garage were two paintings: the authentic, for me to examine, and a copy to take away."

"How do you know?"

"I knew on Wednesday." She smiles at me patiently, as if she was explaining to a kid how her microscope works. "When I first saw the Raphael on Wednesday, I thought it was a fake for sure. I could smell the newness of it—fresh paint, you know? But when I examined it, when I smelled the canvas, I found I was wrong. The painting was authentic. It wasn't new. Yet I could smell fresh paint. The garage was not an artist's studio, so where did the smell come from?"

"The fake was in there too?"

"I hunted it down, and found it in that old chest of drawers."

"Not hidden in any way?"

"Not really. It was under some tissue paper, that's all."

"Mother of Christ."

"I knew then that he would make a switch. I guessed that when we went to pick it up this morning, he would switch them and give us the copy to take away."

"But you re-examined it."

She nods. "He knew I would do that. So he left the original on the easel for me to verify."

"While the fake stayed in the drawer?"

"But this time it was neatly wrapped up."

"In brown paper, without string?"

"That's right. The old lady had wrapped it earlier. When she wrapped the original on the floor in front of us, she wrapped it the same way."

"Then he switched them."

"*She* did, while we had our celebratory drink. It was clever. I had just verified it again, we both saw it wrapped, we even helped a little, and as far as we knew, he gave you the same parcel to carry away."

I shake my head. "But you fooled them, Strachey."

"It only took a minute this morning to verify that the copy was wrapped in the drawer and the painting on the easel was the one I saw on Wednesday. So I used my time in there to unwrap her parcel, swap the contents, and rewrap. Making up the parcel the way she did it was not easy."

She gazes out of my bedroom window, as if there was something out there to interest her. There's nothing this time. No one's sunbathing.

"So," I say, spelling out the obvious just to make sure I got it right. "Before we left, the old lady switched the parcels, not knowing you had switched them first. Leonid thinks that he has the original and we have the fake. But we know—"

"That's right. The interesting question is whether Leonid can tell the difference."

"What do you think?"

"There are no distinguishing marks—they could have given his game away. He will realize only if he can identify one from the other. When the old lady wrapped the painting in front of us, which one was that?"

"The fake—no, the original."

"Could you be sure?"

"What do I know about paintings?"

"Probably as much as Leonid. It's like the visitors in the Hermitage. They see a copy which they think is the original, but they don't question it. If we're lucky, Leonid won't question it either."

"Won't he have someone check it?"

"Not till he returns it to the Hermitage. And then it depends who his contact is—a curator or a security man. The curator should realize, but no one else would. Perhaps no one will ever know."

"Is that possible?"

"It's possible for a while. I suspect Leonid has it out for a month or so on loan, like a library book. For that short period, before the art world wakes up, he can sell it several times. For five million dollars a time."

I walk Strachey down to the lobby, and she heads off to catch a tram back to her hotel. Since there's half an hour before supper, I haul back up to my room and run a bath. Hot brown water splatters on to the porcelain. I come to fetch a fresh shirt from the drawer.

Then that little anxiety begins to eat at me again. You know the one. I walk over to the closet, and find I am tiptoeing carefully across the carpet as if I don't know what it is I am treading on. My brain is twitching. I need to run my hands along the suitbag. I need to reassure myself that everything is fine. So I open the closet door and reach inside.

But of course, it's gone.

19

I snatch open the door and look again. With both hands I pull the clothes aside. I look on the floor.

When I step back, the room is silent. I fill the air with the sound of my breathing.

I do all the stupid things anyone would. I separate the hanging clothes one more time. I check the shelves. I look around the room to see if I put the bag somewhere else. I open drawers. I check under the bed. I hunt in the corners of the room.

But it isn't there.

Wearily, I sink on to the bed. For I don't know how long, my mind jams solid. Then I push myself up on to my feet, and walk slowly round the room one last time, willing the bag to reappear. When I reach the bathroom it is full of steam. The hot tap is still running into the tub, and has filled it with rusty brown water. I turn it off.

I try to think.

But after another long minute, I am no clearer what to do. My stomach has shrivelled to the size of a golfball. I pick up the phone.

She took it calmly. That's how it sounded. Maybe she was as stunned as I am. I don't know. Nor do I know what she said to me. Nor do I know why I phoned her. I had to do something, I guess.

I think she said she was coming back over.

I examine my options. I could report the bag as stolen. But I can't tell them what is inside it. I can't tell them why I am gibbering and chewing the edges of the carpet.

I could do nothing.

There are no other options. Either I report the bag as stolen, and act like it's an ordinary room-theft, or I do absolutely nothing. I just sit here. I fly home to Gottfleisch and . . .

Five million dollars. I have lost him five million dollars. So I have no options. The only thing I can do is report the bag stolen. I remember now: that's what Strachey said.

I look blankly at the phone. One thing is certain: I cannot pick up that ugly piece of bakelite and cry my way round the switchboard to a succession of faceless voices. I have got to see someone. I have got to grab them by their lapels and *plead*.

"I need to see the manager."

The girl behind the desk stares up at me. She shows not a hint of comprehension. So I try again in Russian. She still doesn't react. Then she stands up and walks across to where an older woman slowly thumbs through a pile of dockets. The woman does not rise from her chair. She mutters something. The girl responds. They seem to say the same thing to each other about six times, then the girl returns. "You see Intourist on second floor."

"I need to see the manager."

"Intourist Service Desk is upstairs."

I turn away. We could keep this up all night. I head up the stairs to the second floor.

At the second floor desk sits a blonde matron with epaulettes. There are no customers. I ask to see the manager.

"Name? Room Number? What is problem?"

"I've had something stolen from my room."

"Stolen? You mean a theft?"

"My bag has been stolen."

"What type of a bag?"

"A large one. It holds my suit."

"Your suitcase?"

"No, my bag. I'd like to see the manager. Quickly, please."

"Wait here."

She slides to the other end of the desk and picks up a phone. All the time that she uses it, her eyes never leave my face. Her expression is as if I brought something dirty into her hotel. She slides back.

"Is coming. Wait here."

Two minutes pass. Olga appears. "Good evening," she says. "Can I help?"

"I am waiting to see the manager."

"Is dinner now. Six o'clock."

"Then bring him out of dinner. This is serious."

"Not he that is at dinner. *You* should be. Is six o'clock."

"A bag has been stolen from my room. I want to see the manager."

"I am your representative. When it was stolen?"

"This afternoon. The thief may still be here."

"Why? He is a guest?"

"How do I know?"

"Is most serious. It was stolen from your room?"

The other woman interrupts. "Is not possible. In hotels of Soviet Union we do not have thefts."

I can live without this. "Can we get the police, please?"

Olga says that first she'll take the details.

"Do we have to stand out here?"

She seems surprised. But the customer is always right. She leads me away from the counter to a block of large brown armchairs by the window.

"Isn't there an office—somewhere more private?"

"But why?"

I ask for the manager again.

"He is not available. You must talk to me. I am your representative."

I sit down.

What did I expect of her? She asks sensible questions. She writes down the facts. She does not hurry, because there is no point. The burglary could have taken place any time this afternoon. Charging around the hotel now will achieve nothing. When she has finished with me she will take a statement from the *dezhurnaya*—the keeper of the keys on my floor. It is the *dezhurnaya*'s responsibility to guard the privacy of her rooms. She failed with mine.

Suddenly, Strachey is here.

She whirls in, cool and efficient. She's changed into a pale beige skirt, cream blouse, linen jacket and smart shoes. Her face stays hidden behind her big hornrimmed glasses, and her hair is up in its bun. You'd think she had just stepped in off Wall Street.

Certainly Olga thinks so. She sits stiffly in her chair and bites her

149

pencil. From her Russian clothes, her tall thin frame sticks out like a toe from an old woollen sock.

"Who is this?" she asks through tight lips.

We try to gloss over my exact relationship to Strachey, but Olga will not be put off. She wants every detail she can find. I guess she considers it possible we are working a scam. It's a scam, all right. But someone else has scammed us. I'm humiliated. When Olga makes a note of Strachey's hotel and room number, it's another nail thumped into my coffin. But Strachey is relaxed. She acts like she is my big sister. She speaks in measured tones. Finally, Olga marches off to find the manager. I look at Strachey. She looks at me. We wait.

What do we talk about, now we're alone? What would *you* say? What can anyone say? We stare out the window as glumly as if it were pouring with rain. Commuters down in the street come up from the metro, on to their trams. It is Friday night, the end of the week. But they look the same as always. Head down and get on with it. Can't wait to get home.

Staring out this second-floor window, I am misting it over with my breath. Strachey sits silently beside me. I wipe the glass clear with my sleeve.

Napoleon!

Napoleon Kolesova, who ought to have been incarcerated, strolls out of my hotel front door like he had all the time in the world. The bastard. He steals my picture, then wanders back to gloat.

I leap out of my chair so fast you'd think they just passed two hundred and fifty volts through it. I jump up, smash my knee on the heavy table, curse, and crash past Strachey across the floor. She calls my name. I hammer down the stairs, through the lobby, out the glass door, and on to the pavement. I don't stop. I saw the way he was heading. As I sprint right, I catch a brief sight of him slipping into the metro entrance. He sees me too. One casual glance along the pavement and he jumps like a startled cat.

He moves fast as a cat too.

I hurtle to the metro, slide across the concrete, and approach the five-kopek barriers at the speed of sound. No time for goddamn kopeks. Without fiddling at the slot, I wham straight through.

That was the idea. Because if you thought *I* was moving, you should have seen the machine.

The light beam breaks every time someone enters. The barrier stays open if he paid his coin. Which for 999 out of every thousand passengers makes this a quick and simple way in. But for that one in every thousand, a foreigner bet your life, for that guy the shutters close.

To get from the light beam to the other end of the stall takes me one thousandth of a second. But it only takes a millionth for two steel shutters to flash out and block my way. They sound like a giant's carving knife hitting steel. The quivering blades lock in front of my waist. When I look down my front I expect to see my trousers caught in the mesh. But they're not. I can back away. Passing Russians stare. This kind of behaviour is not allowed. It is "not cultural":

At least two old grundies say I must insert five kopeks and try again. I glare at them. I don't know if I have five kopeks. So I place both hands on the stall and vault across.

Over the floor and down the stairs. I now have half of Mother Russia yelling at me, and I crash down that moving stairway like a soccer hooligan from Moscow Dynamo.

It is pure chance I see anything on the other side. But I do. Just as I hit maximum downward velocity I pick out a face on the other stairs riding up. Slap in the middle of the homeward-bound commuters is Napoleon. He looks smug as teacher's pet on Speech Day.

I slither to a halt on the down stairs, and screw myself round. He is now twenty yards above me, walking up. He has ridden to the bottom, turned round, and come straight back out. He knew I had seen him. And he knew I would follow. Down in the Leningrad metro there is nowhere to hide. You all stand together in that hall.

I do not wait to reach the bottom. We are moving apart too fast. I hop over the moving handrail, and collapse on to the sloping stationary platform between the stairs. I do mean sloping. It is at an angle of fifty degrees. I slither for a grip like I'm a crab on a wet draining-board.

But I clamber across.

I pound up the moving staircase, meeting opposition from the crowd. At the top are no exit barriers. I rush straight out. He has gone.

He may have doubled back to my hotel. But he doesn't know if I was alone in there, and I guess he has run the other way. So do I. I hurtle to my right, round the outside of the metro building, certain I have lost him. He is not in Aleksander Square. He is not in that dull grey nameless lane behind the hotel. He is not on Keronskaya. I keep running.

I pump back round the other end of the long hotel, and then I slow down. There is no point running any more. He could be in any doorway, up any lane, riding any tram along Nevsky. He could be back inside the metro.

As I approach the front entrance I see Strachey waiting on the pavement. We stand in the cool air, dust swirling round our feet.

"Who was it—Leonid?"

"No."

"Yuri?"

I let my brain settle. She doesn't know about last night. Nor about Napoleon, come to that. "It was nothing to do with Leonid. This was another guy. A villain."

She looks puzzled. I tell her I'll explain later.

"I rushed out after you," she says. "But you'd disappeared. Then you burst out of the metro, looked straight through me, and shot off the other way."

"That man I was chasing—when he came out the metro, did you see which way he ran?"

"Which man?"

I give a description, but it means nothing to her. We trudge back into the hotel and up the stairs, back to where we had been sitting. Olga is waiting. With her is an anxious-looking slob who I take to be the manager. He asks some of the questions Olga asked earlier, but is the first person to make an apology. It doesn't help. "Can we get the police?" I ask.

I guess it is the first day in my life I ever *asked* for a cop, and from the manager's reaction he is not too eager himself. He hopes we can settle it without them. "Have you insurance?" Olga asks.

Strachey chuckles ruefully, and I say no, I am not fully insured. *Not for five million dollars, Olga.* Then I decide to hell with it—I need all the help I can get. "I think I know who stole it. Have the police put out a search for a man called Kolesova. I saw him just now."

"Kolesova?" the manager queries. "Where does he live?"

"I don't know."

The manager sighs. "We will check. He has permission to visit hotel?"

"I doubt it."

Olga and the manager exchange glances. The manager stands up. He asks would I mind if he inspected the room now. I say he can. As we troop across the floor I try again to get the cops started on a search for Napoleon. "It will be done," Olga declares. But not yet.

The manager suggests that Strachey waits downstairs. We say no, she comes too. From behind the Intourist Desk, we are watched by three silent clerks. One of them is Natalia. She avoids my eye.

Up on the fifth floor is a new key lady. Before we can reach her desk she has my key out of her drawer. God knows what they did with the *dezhurnaya* there an hour ago, but this one is taking no chances.

The manager fits the key in my door, opens, and we crowd inside. Strachey comes last. The manager mutters something I don't catch. Olga turns to us. She says there may be fingerprints, so don't touch anything.

The room looks the kind of dump it always does. The manager takes a large grey handkerchief from his pocket, walks across and pushes my bathroom door. The light is on. Warm clammy steam hangs in the air. Mirrors drip. The bathtub is full of tepid brown water. He stares at me.

Olga walks into the bathroom and inspects the bathtub. "Did you do this?" she asks. I nod. She places a bony finger into the water, then shakes it dry. "You have a bath?" she asks.

"I was going to."

"This water is cold."

"It wasn't when I put it in."

I pull the plug, and the unused water starts to swirl away. Olga and the manager both watch me as if my action had significance. Then the manager uses his handkerchief again to move the door and peer behind. Nothing.

In the bedroom we stand like lampstands while he wanders around, examining but not touching, as if taking an inventory. He is looking for clues. God knows what he expects to find. Then he asks where my bag had been.

I reach for the closet door, but he stops me. Using his handkerchief, he takes gentle hold of the handle, and pulls the door open. He jerks the other door open too. There are my things, swaying on the rail.

There is the suitbag, swaying alongside.

20

"No," Strachey warns, "not here."

"Why not?"

"I need a drink."

"The drinks can wait."

"I need a drink *now*." She lays her cool hand on my wrist. "You can bring that with you, if you like."

"Strachey—"

"Come *on*!"

And she marches me out of the bedroom as if I was on a lead—Russian manners are catching. I let her haul me up past the *dezhurnaya*, on past the buffet and along the corridor.

"I thought you wanted a drink?"

"Somewhere neutral," she says. "Do you have a buffet on every floor?"

We try the third. She sits in a large armchair, well away from the bar. "I'll hold your bag," she says, "while you fetch the coffee."

I leave her seated among brown leatherette armchairs and low tables, and walk up the other end to the counter in the smart little dining area. The coffee is espresso, and smells as if you might want to drink it. There is food. There are even bottles of wine.

I begin to understand how it feels to live here. You get so used to queues and the endless "not available" that when a few bottles of wine do go on display, you perk up. They're like a surprise gift. Back home, you'd expect a bar full of choice, with all the brand names. You'd think nothing of it. Here, anything new shines out and grins at you. Little things mean a lot.

But I don't buy the wine. I fetch two espresso coffees, two cakes, and two hunks of bread with some cheese. It feels strange to buy two of things.

"That was cheap," I tell her. "Just over a rouble."

"Things *are* cheap here."

"If you can find them."

"Yes."

Which has explored that conversation to its limit. We sit buried in armchairs, sipping hot coffee, wasting time. But I can't wait: I have to see inside that suitbag.

"Where do you suggest?" she asks.

"Not here, it's too exposed. What was wrong with my room?"

"Use your head, Mickey."

I suppose you agree with her. You're slumped there, reading how Mickey Starr lost his Raphael, and you're thinking: who is this berk? Can't he see that someone knew the suitbag had the painting in it, and the only way they knew that was because they saw him put it there? So, you ask smugly—you don't ask gently, like Strachey here—how did someone see you, Mickey? Were they hiding in your room? Was it the Invisible Man?

You're in Russia, Mickey, remember? They bug rooms here, boy. And by the look of what happened, they did not stop at bugging: they put an electronic eye in too. That mirror over the bed, probably. Video camera behind. It seems I've been given the master bedroom—the one where they put the visiting diplomat to romp with naked Soviet startlets. Back home, he gets a surprise pack of holiday snaps, and has a heart attack.

This cannot be happening to me. I am not a diplomat. And where are the starlets?

"Let's walk through this once more," Strachey says. "You hid the painting in the bag, hung the bag in the closet, then you came round the Hermitage with me. We returned together, you saw me out and then discovered the bag was missing. You reported it. While we were waiting, you saw this Kolesova character. You chased after him. We returned to your room. The bag was back."

At least she believes my story. Back in the hotel bedroom, when the goddamn bag reappeared on the rail, there was the kind of silence that, had he been in the bag, you could have heard baby painted Jesus gurgling. The manager and Olga backed out the room like I was drunk. If we hadn't been leaving tomorrow, Olga might have called a Russian shrink. Maybe she thought Strachey was my travelling nurse.

"So your room is bugged and videoed," Strachey muses. "And anything said or done there is down on tape and film."

Which explains why she whipped me out before I could open the bag. And which makes me feel very uneasy indeed. They were watching everything I did. They must have heard some interesting conversations. I phoned everyone—Gottfleisch, Ma and Leonid from there. I even phoned Strachey, tonight. Somebody knows every damn thing I have been doing.

Strachey interrupts my brooding. "We weren't exactly discreet on the phone, were we?"

"Not if they speak English." I try to grin, and fail. "But how does Kolesova fit into this?"

She frowns. "I'm not sure he does," she says. "You'd better tell me about him."

"He's just a petty crook trying to get into the big time."

She studies me. "How long have you known each other?"

"It's a long story. Let's look inside the bag."

"Here?"

I look around. "Why not?"

"I doubt the tea-lady is KGB, but do you really want to open it here?"

"Hell, Strachey, you and I must be the only people who *don't* know whether it's still inside."

I move my armchair so it faces away from both the serving area and the corridor. I unzip the bag. My hand pushes down to the bottom, past my poor old suit, to the little plastic tag. I tear back the Velcro and feel behind the inner lining. "It's still there."

"Let's see it. Anybody who matters has already."

"Maybe he didn't find it. You can't feel it through the lining."

"Of course he found it. That's why he stole the bag."

I tug it free from its hiding-place, and bring it out of the bag. It's the same brown paper parcel, wrapped tight without sellotape or string. A flush of relief floods up through my body. My heart is on overdrive. I want everything to be all right. I don't want anything but that.

"Open it," she says.

I peer over the back of my armchair. No one is passing. The woman behind the counter is turned away, her face twelve inches from a small flickering TV. In the dining area, a middle-aged couple sit eating sausage. Close by them, an old man reads a newspaper in his chair.

The brown paper is tucked up tight. Only its folds hold the parcel together. I unpick one end. The parcel stays tight. I unpick the other end. Then I unfold the flap along the centre, and open it. I peel back the tissue paper.

There lies the Raphael, pretty as a Valentine card. It is unchanged. Strachey leans forward to peer through her hornrims. My mouth is as dry as the canvas. I say, "It's the fake, isn't it?" And she nods. We've been switched.

We agree the following charade.

Up two floors to the fifth, along the corridor to my room. Open the door. Walk in looking happy.

"Thank God we've still got the painting," I say—loud enough for the mike to pick up.

"What do you think happened?"

"It must have been an ordinary room thief. He didn't realize what he had stolen. When we raised the alarm he put the suitbag back and ran away."

"That must be right," she says. "He won't try again."

"You're sure?"

"Pretty sure." Then she smiles as sweet as Madonna and says, "Mickey, I need a bath. I don't want to trek all the way back to my hotel. Can I use yours?"

"Feel free. I'll go for a coffee. You won't be disturbed in here."

Then I re-hang the suitbag on its rail. She turns on the bath.

"I'll see you in half an hour," I say, and I leave.

You with us so far? The room is bugged. Sound and vision, continuous performance. But we aren't supposed to know it. Whoever watches the action is watching us now to see how we react. They want to know if we have realized the Madonna was switched. Or are we so relieved to see her pretty face again, we'll say a thousand Hail Marys and let it rest?

They hope so. That's why they bothered to switch paintings. I am meant to think I still have the original. OK, I'll go along, let them think they fooled me. It's the only way to make them drop their guard. It's the only chance we have to get the real one back.

So why is the lovely Strachey taking a bath?

To prove we don't suspect the hidden camera.

Let's face it: if you knew your every move was on secret video, would you strip off and walk around in the nude? No. So that's why she will. She is gonna parade around that bedroom as innocent and trusting as the virgin in the painting. Somewhere in the basement will be a room with a hundred hairy Russians clamouring round the TV monitor. All I gotta do is listen for their growl.

But I won't. I have other things to do.

Whoever organized Candid Camera in my bedroom did not do so by chance. It was not an afterthought. That kind of electronics is not laid on in every room. In half of these hotel rooms even the ordinary TV doesn't work. If they can't guarantee black-and-white television, what hope is there for cameras? No, it was not coincidence. I was placed there specially.

And by whom?

It can only be by my personal Intourist representative. Every other tour party has one courier: we have two. One does all the donkey-work, knows what she is doing, behaves like you'd expect of her. Natalia just follows me about.

She has trailed me around Leningrad. She tried to seduce me, took me round the nightlife, hovered behind in Petrodvorets. I must have been blind. (And don't tell me you guessed as much, back on page whatever. You're not living this, like I am. You have time to think.) Natalia has kept an eye on me since I arrived. The Russians sussed me out early: single, lonely, five years in jail. Their goddamn London embassy probably dug it out. I see why you apply for visas three months in advance: this man is a criminal, he must be watched.

When I think back, I can see that I have been as open as a guidebook: on the room-phone night and day. Natalia saw where I hid the painting. She was listening in when Strachey told me how she'd foiled the switch. All Natalia needed was time to switch the paintings back. But I didn't give her enough. I saw Strachey out of the hotel and returned to my room immediately—when Natalia was only half-way through. The real painting was out, the fake not yet back in. If I'd come back a little later, I might never have known. I had no reason to open the parcel. I'd go all the way back to Gottfleisch with a fake.

As I may still have to do.

These thoughts take place over a slow cup of coffee on the second floor. In the buffet. Near the desk. Where I can keep an eye on the *dezhurnaya*.

Natalia and Olga's room is along the corridor, past the desk where the *dezhurnaya* sits doing embroidery. She picks contentedly with her needle. It's a napkin or something. She takes her time. She has little else to do. She could be here all night.

One thing I have learnt about these supervisors is that they do not stay at their desks. Like anyone else, they have to take a leak. They have other duties. They have forms to make up. They keep an eye on cleaners, porters and chambermaids. They have the linen room to check.

It does not take long for an ex-con to suss how to break into a Russian hotel room. All he needs is patience.

For now, the *dezhurnaya* is rooted to her desk. She is gonna finish that embroidery. I sip my coffee and nibble chocolate. It tastes like you should cook with it, and it cost a rouble eighty. That's more than I paid for the entire snack I had with Strachey half an hour ago. But food is a necessity, chocolate is not. Luxury is not approved of.

My coffee is finished. I snuggle into the chair with my book.

I read a chapter and a half, and just as I reach the part where the hero meets his girl again in Brighton, the *dezhurnaya* stands up. She has finished her stitching. She lays the material carefully on her desk, she stretches, then she waddles past me up the corridor. I close my book.

Before approaching her desk I wait half a minute. I don't want the counterhand at the buffet to be suspicious. Casual as you like, I do what you always do when the supervisor is away. I stroll round the back of her desk, and open the drawer which holds the room keys. The fobs stare up at me with their numbers clearly shown. I take the one I want.

Room 248 is just a dozen paces away. That's all. I approach the door, glance briefly behind, and fit the key in the lock. I twist it. The door opens. I step inside. I close the door.

The curtains have been drawn across the window, but they are as skimpy as the ones in my room—a feeble screen against the evening light. I glance into the bathroom, turn on the light, and step inside. Nothing is there, except girls' things on the shelf above the wash-basin.

I come out, and step into the main room. There are two single beds. On one of them lies Natalia. She wears a white blouse with the top three buttons open, a red skirt, and no shoes. She has her eyes open. I freeze.

We stare at each other as expressionless as pillows. Her dark hair is tousled and her face looks pale. "What are you doing here?" she asks. When she sits up, her hair tumbles on to her shoulders.

"I came for my picture."

"What picture?" She fiddles with the lower of her three buttons to do it up.

"You know the one."

"I must ask you to leave."

I sit down beside her on the bed. "Where is it?"

"What are you talking of?" She tries to stand up. I place my hand on her shoulder. She stays sat.

"Is it in here?"

"I try to rest. I am tired."

She sounds convincing. I hope I've got this right.

"I have to look here. It's the only place I know."

"What do you mean?"

I stand up, walk over to their closet, and open the door. There is little to see. Between them, the two couriers have less clothes than I have. As I flick through their thin dresses I say pleasantly, "I thought your room would be empty. I should have knocked."

"What do you do with my clothes? Stop that."

"I saw your key in the *dezhurnaya*'s drawer. I thought you were out."

"Is Olga's key."

"Yeah." I move to the bureau. "Where is it, Natalia? Do I have to go through all your things?"

"Please leave immediately." She reaches for the phone.

"Room Service is slow here, isn't it?" I have finished with their lowest drawer. I start the next one up. She slams down the phone, and darts across to me. As she reaches round to grab my arm, I see her face in the mirror. She is angry. I ask, "You got a camera behind this glass too?"

Her grip is surprisingly hard. She snatches my hand from out of their blouses. Just this once I turn on her, so she will know I mean what I say. "Don't play dumb," I say. "I've worked it out." Then I pull the top drawer open.

Russian underwear is substantial. The garments will last. They could hide a maiden's charms, but not a Raphael. Leaving all their drawers open, I walk over to their two shabby cases. "Get out," she spits.

There is no need for me to fiddle with the locks. The cases are empty. I shake them and drop them to the floor. They don't rattle.

The bedside cupboards are too small. Under the beds, the bases are solid. I look around. She wouldn't hide the painting under her mattress, and the bathroom gets too damp. There is nowhere else. "So Kaplan has it," I say.

"Please go now."

I pick up her phone. She watches as I key nine and Leonid's number. We both stand silent as the relays clunk and the call goes through. At Leonid's house it rings unanswered. I let it ring.

"You know where he is?"

She glares at me. She is as unhelpful as the phone. After ten seconds I give both of them up.

"You get a message to him. Tonight. Tell him we did not come here to buy a fake. We want the real thing—now—or we want the money back. It's his choice. One or the other. Tonight. Nothing else."

She stands impassive. But I reckon that just confirms that she knows what I am talking about. Otherwise her mouth would be hanging open. She'd still be fuming. She wouldn't know what the hell was going on.

I know the feeling.

"One other thing," I tell her as I leave the room. "Tell him that if we don't hear from him tonight, we will show the authorities a statement from his foreign bank account. The one with all that Western money. It should put him away for life. If he don't get shot."

*

Strachey looks fresh and clean. But then, she is on television. The room has a residual warmth from her taking a bath. It is cosy. I could stay with her here for a long time.

She has put back on her cream blouse and beige skirt. Her hair remains in its bun, but the back of it is damp. Though she looks up innocently from the chair by my bedside, I can see the question hidden in her eyes.

I shake my head. We can't speak here. "Did you enjoy your bath?"

She shrugs. "I used to be so shy."

I laugh, and we leave the room.

More coffee. More waiting. We examine how things stand. They know that we know that they know we bought the painting. They know that we know they switched it back. We know that they know we have few high cards to play with. But both we know and they know that one of them is an ace—Kaplan does not want us to talk.

Then I tell Strachey where I was last night. Tubby and Elephant mean nothing to her, but she is shocked when I tell her Yuri got himself killed. Leonid's injured arm, she says, is the least he deserves.

"That's what Napoleon thought. He came to the hotel to thank me. Personally."

"Did he take the picture?"

"He knows nothing about it. He came to find what happened to his friends. We can forget Napoleon: he's only interference."

She does not look convinced. She thinks on, sorting things out in her mind. "Natalia is hand in glove with Leonid Kaplan?"

"She has to be. Why else would she switch the picture?"

"This threat you made her about Leonid," she muses. "If he's in thick with the police, his foreign bank account won't matter."

"Those friends were MVD—civil police, local boys. Smuggling and international deals are the province of the KGB. Leonid won't want trouble from them."

"Nor will we."

Which is one hell of an understatement. Back in the comfort of home we can shop Leonid without difficulty. We could send him down for a long cold time. But if it is him who shops us before we gct out of here, we could be the ones for that long cold time. International art theft will not persuade the British government to support our case. They are more likely to agree with the Russians that we should be made an example of. Just don't be *too* hard on them, they'd say.

A moderately severe Russian prison sentence is an experience I do not need.

"It'd make Pentonville seem like heaven," Strachey agrees.

"How d'you know about Pentonville?"

"Gottfleisch told me."

"What else did he tell you?"

"Why you went in. When you came out. Why you are doing this."

"Why am I? Remind me."

"You can't get honest work. You're in debt. Your mother is ill."

"She's dying."

"That's what he said. I wasn't sure if you knew."

"Of course I know."

Our eyes meet. I am the one who looks away. She says, "Don't feel bad. He bought me too."

"In what way?"

"When I left the gallery, he took me on. At twice the salary."

"He pays you wages?"

"And he stamps my card."

"What does *that* mean?"

"Just that. I'm a regular employee. I pay income tax. I have a private pension scheme. I don't sleep with the boss."

"I didn't think you did."

"Some people think so. I don't sleep with anybody now."

"That makes two of us."

"But I'm staying that way, Mickey. Celibacy is the in thing nowadays, didn't you know?"

"Not in Deptford it isn't."

I smile briefly. How someone with her looks thinks she can stay celibate is beyond me. Men must be queuing for her. One of these days her guard will slip. Some lucky hunk will catch her pretty blue eye, and snap will go her celibacy. A goddamn stockbroker, I suppose. Some snot-nosed poncing bigshot. She wouldn't fall for a normal guy like me, who'd look after her, cherish her. I change the subject.

"What has your old man been doing since the Crash?"

"Pottering." At first she looks as if she'll clam up, as she usually does when I ask anything too personal. Then she shrugs, and gives a wry smile. "The first few months he blustered around, trying to pretend that life was the same as before. Then his pace slowed. Then he stopped. Now he digs the garden."

"You want him to go back in the City?"

"He's bankrupt. To go back he'd have to pay a fortune in debt. It's not worth it."

"Who does he owe to?"

"Oh . . . Speculators. People like he was. The City is a big gambling casino, that's all. Most of the time they win. When they lose they cry."

Over her shoulder I see Natalia approaching down the corridor. She still wears the red skirt and white blouse. But now all the buttons are done up, and her hair is tidy. I warn Strachey. Natalia strides to our armchairs and stops. Lazily, Strachey studies her. Natalia looks down at us lounging there. Then she asks, "You have painting to exchange?"

"In this bag." Strachey points to her travel bag.

"No," says Natalia. She points to the suitbag I clasp between my knees. "Is in this one, I think. You must come with me, please."

"Where?"

"You come now, please."

Neither of us move. "Sit down, Natalia," I say. "Where do you want us to go?"

She doesn't sit. She keeps a bored expression on her face, as if she was allocating seat numbers. "We go to sort things out."

Strachey and I have been here for a week. With Russians we have been through the learning curve. We have learnt all we want to learn about their compulsive withholding of information: the way details are only partial; directions are incomplete; signposts are obscure. We know the way that doormen like to say No; the way shops prefer to stay shut; the way cafés close for coffee-break and restaurants shut for lunch. We know how the thing you want is "not available"; what you want to do is "not possible"; where you arc going "will be revealed". And we ain't gonna take it any more.

I spell the words out very slow. "Tell us where we are going."

"I take you to Comrade Kaplan."

"That's better. And where is he?"

"I cannot tell you. I will show you."

"Do we walk, or go by car?"

"A taxi is outside."

"Does the taxi know where to go?"

"I will show him."

Strachey and I exchange weary smiles. Natalia can have this little victory. We know we have broken through.

22

Natalia does her best to confuse us, but we follow the route with Strachey's pocket map. The driver takes us by the Pushkin Theatre, round the back of the Theatre Museum, along the lonely Fontanka Canal to Turgenev Square, past the Kirov and across two small canals, out past the Leningrad History Museum, over the Greater Neva on the bridge that tourists don't use, on to Vasilyevsky Island, across, over the Bolshoi Bridge in to watery Aptekarsky Island, half-way down Bolshoi Prospekt, turn left into the area that Strachey's map gets vague about, across a small bridge, round some narrow alleys, over another bridge so we lose track of which island we're on, round a couple of corners, till we finally pull to a halt on a blue waterside. "This is either the Malaya Nevka or the Srednyaya," she whispers, "—I think."

"When the time comes to go back," I tell her, "we'll call another cab."

We climb out, leaving Natalia to settle the fare. It was her treat. She flashes her Intourist badge at the driver, and he grunts. He produces a pad, and she signs the docket. He rips off a copy and gives it to her. She reads it, nods, and he drives away. "Come," she says.

In the late evening cool by the riverside we set off at a brisk pace. The taxi could have brought us this last one hundred yards, but Natalia didn't want him to know where we were going. Just in case. Never reveal anything.

I had expected somewhere lonely, somewhere dead. The sort of place that isn't hard to find in Leningrad. But this waterside area is alive. Upstairs in a blank-faced house, a party is in full swing. Outside on the railings lean a group of students. In the middle of the broad river a boat passes—music and laughter surging out with its swell. Several buildings have their lights on. You need the lights now, indoors.

Down river, the sun has dropped below the tops of the buildings. Clouds still glow in its embers. The colour of the water changes from blue to grey. Cold air rises from the surface.

The weather is cool and pleasant. A few folk stroll by the river, but the lucky ones are on the water, carousing in boats. Ahead of us is moored a hulk of a thing, garishly lit with bare lightbulbs, strung high. It is crowded. From on board comes the contented sound of a good pub on Friday night, a genial Russian bear, roaring out its one-note song to drown the band.

Natalia walks stiffly. She disapproves. Clustered round the foot of the gangway are her favourite enemies of the people—a dozen bikers, wearing new gear meant to look old, riding old bikes meant to look new. Several of the kids sit astride their machines, racing the engines. The kids have long greasy hair. They sport denim jeans and mock leather jackets. But their teeshirts are clean, their jeans in one piece: both too precious to tear. They have the pseudo-tough look of the boys in *West Side Story*. The Wild Ones finally hit Leningrad.

Part of their street-cred is to be refused entry to the boat. They sway around the quayside, jeering at the bouncers, pleased they are too disreputable to get on. But we three the bouncers let through. Access to highspots is the same the world over: smart clothes and influence, no tykes. Natalia has a word with an Ivan in a tie, and we are on. Behind, the teenagers catcall, impressed by Strachey's shiny high heels clattering on the wood. She steps on deck like a princess boarding the Royal Yacht.

Around the deck, the customers lurch and stagger as if they were out in a force five. They are gonna strut their stuff until they drop.

"First we find a table," Natalia says. It is easily said—like everywhere in Russia, this boat is short of seats. We hunt between the revellers as they reel into each other, till we sneak four chairs. We drag them away to a table at the end of the deck. Natalia stands behind her chair, clapping her hands like a schoolmistress on an outing. Into the evening air she flashes a broader grin than I have ever seen her grin. "Now—drinks!" she cries. "What will you like?"

I ram my hand into my pocket and produce all my remaining roubles. "I'll get the drinks. I've got to get rid of these."

"So many!" Natalia exclaims. "I hope you did not trade on black market."

"Come off that high horse," I laugh, and I thrust notes in her hand. "We've got your number now, Natalia. You're one of us."

"I am Soviet citizen," she starts. But she is stopped by a sudden burst of small explosions. Fireworks fizz into the sky. People clap and cheer. We watch Natalia laughing into the sky. "Is festival of White Nights!" she shouts. "The party will begin."

"But why, Leonid, why do you set off fireworks on the brightest nights of the year?"

"For festivity."

"Fireworks should be in the dark, when you can see them."

"On dark evenings we stay indoors," says Natalia. "Is too cold."

Strachey raises her glass of sparkling wine, and inhales the aroma. "Leningrad looks so beautiful now."

"She *is* beautiful!" roars Leonid. "I love her."

"Just open more floating bars like this," I suggest. "And put something in the shops."

"You did not come to Leningrad under Comrade Brezhnev," Leonid says, emptying his glass as if it were a mug of beer. "On this that man was right. He did not have foolish Prohibition."

"Is not Prohibition," declares Natalia, banging her own glass down. "Is moderation. We have cured alcohol problem. Comrade Gorbachev—"

"Drink and be merry," I cut across her, placing my fingers on her mouth. "No more lectures tonight."

She reaches quickly to take hold of my hand, but for one second before she moves it away, she lets my fingers rest against her warm lips. Slowly she carries my hand down to the table, holding my gaze with her dark brown eyes.

"Gosh!" exclaims Strachey. "Are there more fireworks to come?"

Leonid laughs. "Our bottle is empty," he says. "We must buy more."

I stand the empty in the centre of the table beside the first one. It is the Soviet way. As the evening wears on, all the empties crowd together on the table, reminding you how much conviviality you've been privileged to enjoy.

"First we talk business," I say.

Earlier this evening, when I looked at the cards in our hand, it seemed that all Strachey and I could make was "No Bid". We had one ace—not of trumps—and nothing else. It looked bad. But we played our ace, saying that if Leonid didn't come we'd expose him to the authorities, and it snatched our first trick. Here he sits now, gulping Soviet champagne, belching in his seat like a gorged cherub. Now I try for a second trick: we have finished the second bottle and he wants another. I announce that the next is on me, but not till we finish negotiations. The drink is on me, but the pressure on him.

We must clarify the situation, get every detail clear. Has Leonid still got the painting? If it is back inside the Hermitage, it will not come out. Not tonight. Leonid won't say he has it, and he won't say he has not. I point out that if he hasn't, we can all go home to bed, and he can wait till he hears the knock on the door at dawn. So he says he has it. I ask where. He won't say. I say that unless he does, I shall assume he hasn't got it, and telling me where it is can't hurt, because he has me right here in his sight. He says he has the painting stashed. I ask how easily he can reach it. He says he can fetch it in half an hour.

OK, I say, if you still have the painting, do you have authority to sell it? He says to sell it would be a treasonable offence. I say I know this, but can he sell it? He shrugs. I ask if we are wasting our time here. He says no. He can sell.

I am taking it for granted, I say casually, that there is no problem on the price.

He pulls a face and tries to hedge, but I cut in. I explain I am not going to phone home and rouse friend Gottfleisch to say the price is up again. A deal is a deal. Leonid squirms on his chair, but price is not the problem. He wanted to palm us with a fake. And got caught. Twice.

Let us look on the bright side, I suggest. We've had the frantic runaround, but now we can all come out on top. If I get the genuine picture, he can keep five million dollars. Which is already one million more than he expected. If he stays lucky, maybe Gottfleisch would like to trade again. Comrade Kaplan could be an ex-pat millionaire. Several times over.

"I do not want to leave Soviet Union."

So be a millionaire at home. But let's remember: if we do not get either the picture or our cheque back, we will have to inform Comrade Gottfleisch that we just lost him five million dollars. He will then give Strachey and me a most unpleasant time. But we'll survive. Then we will send the Soviet Embassy several clear copies of Lenny's Swiss bank statement, together with a helpful letter, and when the Soviet authorities check it out, they will give Lenny an unpleasant time as well. But unlike me and Strachey, he will not survive.

On the one hand then, we can all lose. On the other hand, we can win. What we must do now, sitting around this rickety table, is choose which. It is not a difficult decision. And I think that if he was going to cheat us again, he would not be here.

"We are not buying your fake, Lenny, you understand that?"

"I understand."

"So which are you gonna give us— our cheque back, or the real Raphael?"

"I will collect painting," he says, and we all sigh.

"Now the thing is, Lenny," I continue, never a one to flinch from kicking a man when he is down, "the thing is this. You have put us through some wicked aggravation. And we were good to you. We coughed up extra money. Not to mention that I helped you with Kolesova's mob. So the thing is, Lenny," and here I grin at him with all my teeth, "since we did all this for you, what will you do for us in return?"

Leonid looks glum. Strachey—who sits beside him and is therefore outside his breadth of view—she looks at me as if to say "You've got a nerve. You were sitting there with nothing in your hand, and now you are bluffing a full house." Maybe *you* are thinking much the same. But I tell you: you don't get nothing in this world unless you ask for it, and the best time to ask for it is when he is up against a wall. And the time he is most up against that wall is when he thinks you've just done him a favour. He feels he ought to do something for you in return.

Exactly what Leonid can do for me I have no idea. It is for him to work out. All I've done is shift the game. The trick I had to win was to get him to re-exchange the paintings. This is now agreed. We have progressed from there on to finding something *else* he can concede. I don't care what that is—he can buy the next round of drinks—all I care is that the main point is settled and left behind.

"What we do is this," begins Natalia. I thought she was just spectating, and I look to her with surprise concealed. "We will guarantee safe exit from Soviet Union. Tomorrow you fly out safely and take it home."

I let this sink in.

"No monkey business with the painting? We get the real thing?"

"Agreed."

"I get it back to the hotel with no accidents?"

"Agreed."

"No one breaks into my room and removes it again?"

"Agreed."

"What are you gonna do—sit up all night watching through my mirror?"

Her lips droop. "Is not funny."

"And tomorrow I get it to the airport, through Customs, on to the plane, and fly home with no problems?"

"I guarantee."

"Just how are you able to do that?"

She shrugs. "Customs, they do not really check you. You are tourist. For each plane they inspect cases for only two passengers."

"And I could be one of them."

"I will come with you. I will tell them who to check."

"Are you saying that Intourist tells the Customs which cases to open?"

"We know you better than Customs do."

I sit back in my chair. Suddenly I am aware that outside of our little knot of concentration at this end of the deck, festivities continue. Music is playing. Some couples dance. Some tables sing. On their way to and from the bar, people collide without caring. On every table, clusters of bottles huddle tightly in the centre, clinking as the boat sways. In the grey light, the river is choppy. A

173

twelve-foot motor-boat chugs past, crowded with old people waving to us. On shore, strollers saunter at the water's edge. Teenagers on the quay chase each other. They run from their bikes to the wall, from the wall to their bikes, to and fro. To and fro.

"One thing," Leonid says—and here he shows that he too knows something about making deals—he too knows when to ask for something in return: "If we do this extra thing for you, Mikhail, what will you do for us in return?"

I take a breath to think of something, but I don't have to. He carries on: "It must be this. You do not tell Comrade Gottfleisch *anything* about our little difficulty. I want to trade with him again. Is agreed?"

"It's a deal."

"You promise?"

"It's a promise. Now can we fetch the painting?"

"We drink a toast."

He has waited long enough. I'll get another bottle.

"Shampanskoye!" I shout, and I thump the bottle down. White froth oozes out the top. Natalia giggles.

"Carelessness is not approved of," laughs Leonid, grabbing the bottle and waving it over our empty goblets. Most of the wine lands inside them. We hold on to our wet glasses while he stumbles to his feet to make a toast. His left arm is still in its sling, his right fist is wrapped round his drink, so he must stand up without using his hands. On a rocking boat with half a bottle of champagne inside him, this is easier said than done.

"A toast: to Vladimir Ilyich Lenin—may his words live for ever!"

I'll drink to most things, so that one goes down.

Natalia jumps up. "Lenin lived. Lenin lives. Lenin will live for ever!" Down goes that one too.

Strachey is up. In her smart linen jacket she could have stepped off a poster: the scrubbed-clean idealized revolutionary. "To the glory of Art, and the doom of art dealers!" Number three gone. My turn. I say the first thing that comes into my head: "A new world, and a new beginning. Let freedom ring!"

We gulp that one down too, and stand moist-eyed, dreaming of new beginnings in our own individual ways. "Let's dance," I say to Strachey, and we do.

Well, why not? There's no point rushing off for the painting. Either we will get it or we won't. We have played our meagre cards. Far better now to lead Strachey by the hand through crowded tables, up to the small square of deck where couples dance. I turn to face her. In the evening light, her cheeks seem pale. Her lips are parted, and for one strange moment she seems vulnerable, even afraid. But then she smiles, her expression lightens, all her gloss slips back in place. When she floats towards me, her blonde hair brushes my cheek, and I hold her in my arms for the first time.

All around the deck, fairy lights bob up and down on their strings. The moon rides high in the aluminium-coloured sky. As I breathe in her fragrance she whispers, "Do you trust him?"

"We have no choice."

"What if he cheats us again?"

The music is sorrowfully sentimental. Strings surge and sob. Balalaikas trill.

"He won't cheat us now."

"But will you get through Customs, as Natalia says?"

"If not, I'll spend a hundred years in jail and think of what might have been. I've done it before."

"What sort of might have been?"

I won't answer that. It is dangerous. I let more music fill the pause, then say, "They can't stop *you*, anyway. They can prove nothing against you. If I don't get through, send me a postcard."

She squeezes my arm. She is flying on to Yugoslavia. Her package was three days in Moscow, four in Leningrad, then a week in Dubrovnik. It could be a nice holiday after Russia: a week in the sun to help recover from the shock.

"You coming back to London after that?"

It is her turn to let the balalaikas play. When she does reply, she seems to be talking more to herself than to me. Her voice is deeper, without its usual brisk confidence. She could be murmuring to her reflection in the water.

"I haven't decided. I might stay on the Adriatic in the sun. I don't want to go home and watch my parents growing old. I don't know what my life is for."

I try to draw her closer, but it doesn't work. Her body is here, in a soft kind of way. But Strachey is somewhere else. She is hiding. I don't know where.

And when the music stops, we all clap. As we pick our way back through the tables, she is like an actress coming on from the wings. With each step she grows fractionally taller, as if the cool river air helps her to reflate.

Leonid and Natalia are well down that bottle. When we arrive opposite them at the table, I suggest we leave.

"Is no hurry," Leonid protests. I say there is.

"You have not dance with me," says Natalia. "Is our last night."

Leonid agrees. "We go when you come back. Straight away."

"Don't buy another bottle," I tell him. I lead Natalia for her dance.

Unlike Strachey, Natalia has brought her body with her. But I seem to have left mine the other end of the boat. When she presses against me I don't respond.

Five minutes later, back at the table, the party has ended. The bottle is empty. Strachey seems withdrawn. Leonid looks flushed, as if maybe he made a pass at her. It was his only chance. But he heaves himself up, flashes his clerical smile, and bows to me. "Now we go. I go in my car to fetch paintings. You walk with Natalia to flat. I meet you there."

There is an awkward pause. As you might expect.

"You disappearing?"

"Why not? You do not trust me?"

"I'd feel better if we come along."

"You think I do not come back?"

"Let's do it the easy way, Lenny."

"This is easy way. Painting, she is other side of Leningrad, in Baltiskaya. My flat is near—ten minutes' walk. Natalia will make you tea."

"We'll come with you."

"Is not possible."

"Nothing's possible in this damn country! We'll come with you."

"Is not possible because back of my car is filled of boxes. Is not room."

"I'll sit in front. Strachey can go with Natalia."

He sighs theatrically. "So you do not trust me. OK. But if I want to trick you, why do I come on boat? I could have stayed in hiding."

"You're both right," says Strachey, picking up her flight-bag. "I'll go with him. You walk round with Natalia."

"You with him?"

"You with Natalia?" she mimics. "I can't face a stiff walk at this time of night."

So that's that. It'll take them at least twenty minutes to collect the painting and take it to Leonid's flat, so Natalia and I stay on board while they leave the boat. At the foot of the gangway, they have to joss with the bikers. But there's no trouble. They walk with a wave to his car.

It's that same heap of yellow Moskvich, sinking into the tarmac. Leonid unlocks the passenger door, lets her in, walks back round, opens his own door, and with his one good arm, gives us a last wave.

Something moves in the shadows.

I don't know why I noticed. Plenty is happening down there —bikers larking about, stray walkers. Maybe he was the only one in the shadow. Maybe he was the only furtive one. Maybe I've learnt to notice hoodlums like that.

"Napoleon!" I yell.

But Leonid is into his car, slamming the door. Napoleon scurries away from him, close to the wall. I see Leonid switch on the ignition, and I flinch for the bang. It doesn't happen. The car jerks peacefully away, and limps off along the quay.

But Napoleon has slipped into a shiny black Chaika limousine. It purrs into life immediately, and cruises comfortably along the quay in the wake of the stupidest yellow Moskvich that ever was made.

I dart forward.

Half the slobs on this boat are too drunk to get out the way. Hands full of alcohol, they sway into my path, thinking I'm as merry as themselves. One tries to embrace me. Others curse as I crash past their tables. Near the top of the gangplank I trip, stumbling half to the deck before grabbing the rail. I slither down the bouncing gangplank and jump on to dry land.

Two hundred yards away, Napoleon's Chaika is disappearing round a corner. I don't stop running. From the mêlée of teenagers I choose the one with the biggest bike. He stands by it laughing. He falls reeling to the ground.

I jump across his heavy machine and kick it into life. As I surge forward I feel a clump into my back. Two arms wrap round my ribs. When I turn to shake them free, I see Natalia. Her forehead grazes my cheek. With eyes blazing, she leans back from me and yells "Go!"

I go.

Along the riverside we roar, without a car in sight. I head for the corner where I saw the limo turn. But Natalia heaves on my arm and screams "Turn right" in my ear. As we approach the first corner she calls "Here!"

She knows Leningrad. I don't. I slew to the right, leaning low to pull the bike round. She leans with me. She has ridden a bike before.

At the end of the alley I expect to turn left, so we can cut the corner to make ground on the others. But Natalia presses her mouth hot against my ear and says "Right again." I obey.

Now we are on another stretch of river. As far as I can work out, we are hammering away from where Leonid and Strachey went. But Natalia knows where Leonid is going. We cling to the water-side. Where a tributary cuts in from the main river, the road veers inland. We ignore it, and take a sharp left over the tributary. We bump across a bridge and continue down the quay. Then she screams "Left", and I do as I am told.

Across another bridge, on to a wide straight road running inland. I open the throttle. At the next three crossings we have right of way. At the fourth we just take it. The streets are almost empty as we approach maximum speed. Too bad if lights are against us. Natalia wants a Right.

I start to turn.

I think the lights were red. But I shoot through to turn right like she said. There's one problem: we English drive on the left. Right-turns abroad can confuse us. It confuses me. I screw the big bike out into the middle of the road, turning into the left-hand lane like I'm used to. It is full of traffic. Coming at me.

A rackety blue bus is a millimetre from my nose. There is no way back, so I don't complete the turn. I keep going.

We bump up the far kerb. As we scream toward the wall we lean hard to our right, parallel to the pavement. We force the bike around, and hammer down the pavement on the wrong side of the street. A main shopping street. We can't rejoin the road because of traffic.

Ahead is another bridge. A big one.

I choose my moment. One gap, and we bump down on to the tarmac and tear across the street through approaching traffic. A Lada has a heart attack. A lorry hits its brakes. We steam on to the bridge with the wind slapping into our eyes and a T-junction ahead.

By now I don't care. Natalia shouts "Left, now right," which follows the main route and is easy. Though there must have been a traffic light. I guess. We are left again, accelerating. "Left!" she screams. Again we cross a bridge, into a blast of cold air.

We have been here before. Not on this trip, but earlier, coming out. If I had half a second to think, I might recognize where we are. But Natalia is shouting directions fast. I mean fast. We are in a maze of little byways, and we turn at every corner. We shoot small bridges, slither three sides of a square, we kill another Lada and screech up to a main road.

Turn right. Use the *right*-hand lane.

"Stop. Wait here."

I pull over. The engine throbs. I look up along the street, and nothing is happening. Above the engine roar I shout, "Where are we?"

"Sadovaya Ulitsa. We should be in front of them."

I look again along the road. Nothing yet.

"Comrade Kaplan, he use main roads—Kirovsky Prospekt, then Sadovaya. Your Kolesova can do nothing there. He will follow and wait."

She is right. Because appearing down this road from behind us is a sedate little yellow Moskvich, then a gap, then a large black car. I am stepping off our machine when suddenly another bike snarls out of the side street. And another. Then another. Five heavy bikers cruise up to hem us in.

By now, Leonid is upon us. I barge through the motorbikes to yell at him. Strachey sees me. She nudges him. As the car passes, she is within arm's reach through its glass window. Leonid turns, making the Moskvich veer towards the kerb. He clutches the steering wheel with his good hand, and stares at me. I point back to Napoleon. Leonid looks behind. His car oscillates by the kerbside. Then he turns front again and puts his foot down. The engine note changes, but little else happens. I see Strachey peer out the back window as the Moskvich chugs away.

The bikers clutch at me, shouting. Then Napoleon passes, and swings his black Chaika in at us. We jump back. A bike crashes over. For one instant in the confusion I meet Napoleon's eyes. They are narrow slits, darkly glinting against olive skin. He cruises on.

I try to force my way back toward my motorbike, but the teenagers block me in. Everyone shouts in Russian—Natalia more than most. She stands astride the pillion, giving hell. Two lads strain at my arms. I step left, stab my heel on to a toe, and I twist. That frees one arm. I use it to sink a low blow in the other guy's belly. That frees two arms. I step on to the bike.

Which wakes the others. They see now that they didn't try hard enough. But I am on the bike again with Natalia, and I accelerate away.

The two cars storm towards Turgenev Square. Then, as they lurch anti-clockwise into it, Napoleon tucks into Leonid's tail-lights.

But I am catching up. Napoleon knows it's time to act.

At the right of the square is an exit. As the two cars pass it, Napoleon slams into the front off-side of the trundling Moskvich to send it skewing past the exit, on to the pavement. It slams sideways into the wall. I veer left, to avoid the pair of them. Suddenly the bike seems alone in the square. It is as if we passed them in a race.

I pull round into a slithering about-turn. The tyres protest.

Natalia grips me tighter than rigor mortis. For one second, caught between hurtling one way and the next, we are stationary. We stare into a momentary snapshot of the square. Then it shatters with movement.

As Napoleon leaps out of his black car, the bikers roar into the square. Napoleon starts towards the crumpled Moskvich. The bikers screech to a stop. Through their splintered Moskvich windscreen. I see Leonid trying to restart. Strachey is blurred behind the glass.

Between the two cars, Napoleon runs the few short yards. He raises his arm. He carries a stubby automatic rifle and he points it at the screen.

The teenage bikers see the gun, and they slide their machines apart. The square is filled with their noise.

Like a horse from its stalls, my bike leaps forward. It howls towards Napoleon's back. He hears it coming. He glances round across his shoulder and starts to fire. I have startled him. As he spins round, his gun keeps firing, but the barrel tilts high. He holds it too loose. It flutters in his hand, spraying bullets in an arc through the air. When he turns to face me, he brings the barrel down. My front wheel hits him. He flips backwards, arms akimbo, as my bike rears up to mow him down. We thump into his crotch, and blaze on across his chest.

The bike bucks beneath me as I haul it to a tumbling stop. I turn it round. When I inch the machine towards them, my arms begin to shake.

Kids are sprawled across the street. Bikes are on their sides. One has its engine racing, and the whole machine spins slowly on the tarmac as if sucked into a whirlpool. All the riders appear to be moving. But Napoleon lies still.

Inside the Moskvich nothing moves.

Still I walk the motorbike forward. Daylight is growing dim. Behind me, I feel Natalia dismount. She runs past me to the car.

The driver's door opens.

Leonid has twisted in his seat to open it with his right hand. He has not been hit.

I get off the bike. I turn it off. Natalia puts her fingers on Leonid's cheek.

The passenger's door remains shut. Around me is the continuous groan of running engines. They sound like the blood that is roaring in my brain. Natalia says something to Leonid. She uses her right hand to support his arm. I have time to study them, to see how they act at this moment together. I can note with the dead curiosity that stifles other thoughts how her gesture is perfunctory. They are not lovers. I had thought perhaps they were.

Then Natalia turns away from him, and reaches into the car. She stoops under the arch of the door to give her hand to Strachey, clambering out. I am at the rear fender of the Moskvich, and I stop. Like an old lady, Strachey slowly straightens. She clings to Natalia's sleeve, but she does not look at her. She looks at me.

We are aware of no one else in the whole city.

She says in a flat voice, "My door wouldn't open. It hit the wall."

Gently, Natalia releases her. Strachey falters. I step forward. She hobbles two paces, then falls forward into my arms.

When I look up to see what else is happening, a kind of order has returned. Leonid stands by the inert Napoleon. Natalia has led the bikers on to the pavement and is telling them to go home. Some want to argue. But she controls them. It is like they're back at school again, and she is the teacher who can't be brooked. When she produces the card from her pocket, the boys give up. It seems Intourist has a lot of clout. They skulk off muttering to their bikes.

Natalia joins Leonid by Napoleon's body. He will not get up. A small puddle of blood lies in the road around his face, but it isn't moving. We are looking at the corpse of a man I have killed.

Out of the dusk, a solitary car creeps into the square. Leonid behaves like an injured policeman, and waves it past. The driver gawps. But he doesn't stop. Then Leonid walks across to us. "We must leave before police come. I will drive."

I kick the Moskvich. "Will this thing work?"

"I hope."

He slips inside and starts the engine. It fires first time. While he sits in the front, knocking out the shattered windscreen, I suggest we use the Chaika instead.

"Is hire car, in name of Kolesova. We cannot use."

I help him pull splinters from around the frame. He tells us to stand clear so he can test the steering. While he reverses, Natalia walks over with Napoleon's AK47. She says, "You go now."

"Aren't you coming?"

"I stay."

"We must get away from this."

"I will deal with it."

"You can't stay here. The police will be here any minute."

She gives a tired smile. "I *am* police."

I don't say anything. Something about this country has dulled my brain. If I was this slow in Deptford, I'd be a dustman.

Leonid clanks forward in his Moskvich. "Is good as new."

"For a Moskvich, I guess it is."

"Oh, Mikhail, is not so bad. But I am afraid you must both come in through my door."

He climbs out to let us in. I tell him to take Strachey to her hotel first. I can wait.

"You not want painting?"

I'd forgotten about that. What I need now is a week in bed.

In Leonid's flat we open our parcel on the floor. The false Madonna gleams up at us, none the worse. "Is very good," Leonid says wistfully. "Maybe *this* is real one. I cannot remember."

"It is long past midnight," I say. "I stopped laughing yesterday."

He turns to Strachey and throws his arms wide. "What do *you* say?"

"I'm tired too."

He sighs, and stands up.

"It is a good fake," Strachey admits. "An excellent copy. But it's a fake, none the less. We want the real one."

Leonid looks tired too. He heaves himself off the carpet, and trudges out into the next room.

"Is he gonna try another fast one?" I ask quietly.

"I hope not."

We sip our glasses of tea—the colour of strong beer, but hot and sweet. Leonid said that tea was better than coffee for preventing hangovers. He should know.

He returns with something loosely wrapped in soft cloth, and places it beside the copy on the floor.

I say that I thought he kept his pictures ready wrapped.

"Only in shop hours." We smile.

When he has opened his parcel, the two Madonnas lie side by side. I study them briefly. There seems to be some kind of difference between them. I think there is. Hung on a wall separately they would both convince me, but side by side I sense they are not quite the same. Strachey picks up the one that Leonid has just brought in. She holds it several ways to the light, sniffs at it, studies the reverse side.

"Try by the window," I suggest. She smiles. I realize that White Night or no, it is now pretty damn gloomy outside. She has her gear with her anyway. Out comes the ultra-violet lamp. She asks for a socket. Up gets Leonid to plug the thing in.

"Will you need an hour again?"

"No. Last time I had other things to do."

She smiles lazily, and turns the lamp on.

"You are absolutely damn positive?"

"There can be no doubt. Look through the magnifier."

"It means nothing to me."

"Trust me, Mickey. I know what I'm doing."

I put my hand on her shoulder. It's so rarely we have touched. "Of course I trust you," I say.

"Good." For just a moment she rests her hand on the back of mine. It feels cool. "I am satisfied," she tells Leonid.

He releases his breath, and smiles. "Is treasure of Soviet Union."

"Don't start that again," I say.

Strachey stands up. "I'll wrap it myself, if you don't mind."

"You still not trust me?"

"I can wrap things the Russian way."

"I remember."

She is playing it light and easy. But from this moment, she never lets the painting out of her hands.

Until she gives it to me.

When Leonid drops me at my hotel, I am clutching the Raphael to my breast. We dropped Strachey five minutes ago. We couldn't say much of a goodbye with Leonid sitting there. I just squeezed her hand. She squeezed mine back. Then she kissed me. Briefly. On the cheek.

Now Leonid stops the battered Moskvich in the empty hotel forecourt, and we look across the tramlines to the Neva in the dusk. It is as dark now as it will get tonight. The city is quiet.

After hauling around Leningrad at two in the morning in a car with no windscreen, I am not in the mood for long farewells. My face feels like it is back from a week in Siberia. However that feels. It is something I hope I will not find out.

"This is goodbye, Mikhail."

"Yeah. You're a tricky bastard, Leonid, but you're OK."

"It was wrong of me. But you understand: tourists are to take money from. We hope you are easy game—I did not thank you, Mikhail."

"For Napoleon?"

"For Kolesova, yes. And his gang. He is criminal, you know."

"What about this five million dollars, Lenny? That's an awful lot of money. You trust Gottfleisch not to cheat you?"

"I must. Is planned. Tomorrow I fly to Belgrade before Comrade Gottfleisch change his mind. He is your 'tricky bastard' too, I think."

"That's what I think, too. Listen, when you get to Belgrade, why don't you come over to the West? You'll be rich."

"Soviet Union is my country. I want to live here."

"That guy Kolesova—what did he want?"

"He wanted too much. That is trouble with capitalism, is it not? Never are you satisfied."

"Are *you* satisfied?"

"Not yet." He laughs quietly into the night air. "These are exciting days, Misha, a time of change. In Britain, you will think of us sometimes, yes?"

"I won't forget."

"In Soviet Union we will make mistakes. Sometimes you will think we do everything wrong. But it is because we change. That is all. Sometimes things will look more bad than they are, but do not be fooled. These are changes for good." He turns to look me in the eyes. "Goodbye, Mikhail. You are my friend."

"Yeah. Well, goodbye, Lenny. I'll be seeing you."

"No, you will not be seeing me." He shakes his head. He chuckles softly, a little sadly. "Is not possible, you know? Unless you come back one day."

That you will never see someone again is a hell of a thing to say. You might as well say they are dead. Through the dim light we look into each other's faces. Then he pulls me into a warm Russian hug.

"I am your friend, Misha. You remember."

23

We are waiting at Leningrad airport to check in for our return flight. Here we must exchange our last rouble notes and small coins. We buy coffees, soft drinks and sweets. The small range of souvenirs costs twice what they would in *Gostiny Dvor*. It doesn't matter. It's the only way to stop our roubles degrading into worthless scraps of paper.

Sammy still has a hundred of the things. If there was a charity box he would use it. The unknown benefactor. But there is no box. They have had more national disasters in the last four years than England has won football matches, yet there's no charity box. The roubles stay in his pocket.

He should care. He bought two hundred roubles for forty pounds. Out of that two hundred he spent one hundred. So he spent sixty for free, even if he has to flush the remaining hundred down the pan.

Maybe there's an airport sewerman who dredges through the sludge. The spirit of enterprise: where there's muck there's money.

People have their travelling faces on. Wait, step forward, wait, step forward, wait. All morning. They're resigned to it. I'm not. I am not switched off.

Because we are not through Customs yet.

Our main luggage is still with us. It will be checked alongside us before we board. That way they can see whose case is whose. They can watch our faces.

When they take it away we will be left with hand luggage and a packed lunch. No one will eat the lunch. We've seen inside those brown paper bags. Another Russian souvenir.

With the time difference, we should be back in Britain in time for a proper lunch.

*

Stand in line for departure. Kick the suitcases along the floor. Watch what happens.

Given the size of Leningrad, this is a small airport. Just three check-in desks. Five million people live in this town, but I guess they don't do much flying. Around me, people realize that they will not see each other again. Addresses are exchanged, promises made. The queue shortens.

At this desk I should have no problems. This is not where they'll come. Out here, the woman checks our tickets, weighs the luggage, lets us through. Then we carry our suitcases to the walk-through X-ray. Strachey would have been interested, if she was here: how does Madonna look under airport X-ray? I watch. You always do, to see how the contents of your bag photograph: the pair of scissors, razor, bits you can't identify. Madonna doesn't show. All I can see as the suitbag slides through is the hook from my coat hanger.

Beyond the X-ray, Customs men wait by their tables. I can't see Natalia. An officer points to an Irishwoman's suitcase. It goes on to the table, and is opened. Natalia said there would be just one more. The man points.

On to the table goes Sammy's suitcase. It had to be his. And he knew it. Even if he could find anything worth smuggling out, he told me, he'd leave it behind. Or use someone else's case. The trouble with looking like he does is that he's always picked out.

While the uniform rummages, Sammy hovers alongside. He looks guilty, because he doesn't care. He dangles like a large anarchistic puppet, waiting to dance. He grins at me.

That's two cases checked, Natalia.

We are through. Just as she said, they checked only the two cases. They glanced at visas. They waved us on.

Now we wait again, this time in a bleak ante-room without facilities. I sit on a bench and drape my five-million-dollar suitbag across my knees. Sammy flops down beside me.

"The obligatory Russian wait," he says.

"They like queuing."

"No, they just put up with it. You notice how the bus was timed to get us here an hour before we were due? Because it might break down. Or there might be roadworks. Nothing must stop the plane leaving on time, so we leave the hotel an extra hour early. It doesnae matter if the passengers are inconvenienced. We're no customers, we are freight. Planes carry freight, and planes fly on time. The State's job is only to make sure the freight arrives in good condition."

"Arrives where?"

"They havenae worked that out yet. That's the problem."

It is only when we walk out of the ante-room on to the airport concrete that I see Natalia. She stands between two chunks of heavy Russian beef. Her hair is scraped back and she wears a formal brown jacket.

She strides forward. "Good morning, Comrade Starr."

I can't help a tiny shiver, but I give her my brightest smile. "Did you get any sleep last night?"

She sighs. "They ask many questions. Let us walk to your plane."

Everybody has to walk, because the authorities have not supplied a bus. A hundred yards across the concrete stands the Tupolev 154. We drag across in an untidy gaggle, inhaling the last of our Russian air. Habitual commuters shoot ahead: either they can't wait to leave or they want a window seat. Natalia pulls me away from the others. But we continue walking towards the plane. I keep my eye on it. I don't let it out of my sight.

With my suitbag slung casually over my shoulder, I ask, "You *are* letting me on to this plane, Natalia?"

"Why not?"

"I don't like the look of your friends. Your MVD heavies."

"Not MVD for foreign visitors. We are KGB."

"We?"

"Of course. But you knew that already."

"I knew you were police, not KGB."

"I am assigned to look after you. To keep you safe."

"Safe?"

"That is why I have kept so close to you. You are valuable to us, Comrade Starr. We make sure nothing happens to you."

I feel deflated. "How about Leonid—is he KGB?"

189

She seems genuinely amused. "He is—how you say?—exporter. He brings Soviet Union much hard currency. A good man."

"Are you saying this painting is an officially approved export?"

She waves her head in one of those Russian gestures. "Not official, but approved. We need hard currency. Is valuable here."

"And the KGB turns a blind eye for the sake of five million roubles?"

"Dollars, Comrade Starr, not roubles." We both smile at the familiar correction. "But this is not official KGB operation. Just a few of us."

"Private enterprise?"

"You could say so. But it is good for Soviet Union, don't you think? We introduce more hard currency to our economy. Comrade Kaplan, you know, he sells other things too."

"Such as?"

"Is best you do not know."

"You can tell me, Natalia."

"Is not possible."

We slow to a stop on the grey concrete. Twenty metres away, passengers start climbing the metal stairs into the plane. I watch them, warily.

"I didn't know there were women in the KGB, Natalia."

"Oh, you Westerners! We all have same opportunities in Soviet Union. Our sex, religion, race does not matter."

"How about Jews?"

She ignores this. "More than half professional workers in Soviet Union are women."

"Is that a fact?"

"Sixty-one per cent. Women often are higher grade than their husbands—and they earn more."

"Are you married?"

She seems to find that an extraordinary question. "No."

"D'you like working for the KGB?"

"I love my country. I love my Party. As a young girl, I was in *Komsomol*, then army. Now I work in Committee for State Security."

"The KGB?"

"*Da*, KGB. We work to improve international co-operation."

"Co-operation! The KGB are thugs. Everyone knows that—even Russians."

"Your Western propaganda! You think Soviet people hate their life here, don't you? You think we hate our system, and you think we hate the West. We are such a threat to you. How can you believe that we hate both our government and yours? We could hate one, but not both."

I consider this. Then I look at her and say, "Is not possible."

She grins. She grins up at me like a high-school kid, like one of those breezy *Komsomol* girls striding out in sports kit. "Perhaps you begin to understand," she says.

The last stragglers are climbing into the plane. She leads me to the foot of the steps.

"We hope to see you again, Comrade. We always are happy to trade with the West. *Do svidan'ya, Tovarishch!*"

LONDON

24

I should have guessed they would meet me at the airport. Not Gottfleisch himself, of course—just a couple of trusties. Because they do not want to attract attention, they act affable. As long as I stay within touching distance, they will try to smile. Their eyes are as hard as their teeth.

I glance around the airport terminal as we stride through. There is so much colour. There are all these kiosks selling things. It looks smart.

We step out into British weather: cloudy, dullish, like an evening in Leningrad. Their big Rover is parked close by in the short-term car park. While we walk across, they don't talk. They must be practising for a job in Russia. I ignore them. Inside the short-term it is crammed with shining cars. I want to stroke their beautiful bodies. Even the smells are different. I am about to walk round to the rear of the Rover to stow my case when they say No: something that valuable should travel inside. "How about my suitbag?" They say it can ride in the back. I shrug. I don't put them right.

I lay the precious suitbag gently on the interior carpet. It seems to cling to the surface pile. I am as careful with it as if I were lowering Baby Jesus on to the soft mattress of his cot. They slam the lid. Philistines.

I climb into the car and settle into the back seat. Carefully, the two hunks wedge my case of dirty laundry into the front, and strap it in with the seatbelt. Then one of the trusties climbs in the back with me, and the other drives us off. We look like an amateur taxi.

I decide to make conversation. "Anything happened while I was away?"

The driver says nothing. The heap beside me grunts.

"Listen beanbags," I say. "We are supposed to be on the same side. This is not a collection job."

Which makes me remember my own collection job—the one I

did before I left. It also reminds me that this is an organization I am getting out of. This is not how I wish to spend my life.

I ask what happened to Calvin.

Maybe travelling makes me cussed. Maybe I think I deserve a better welcome. But I don't feel helpful anymore. I let them lead me into Gottfleisch's sitting-room. It has a thick pinkish carpet and is full of antiques. Paintings hang on the walls. They look like those dark landscapes stacked up in the Hermitage. I let the hulks plonk my big suitcase in the middle of the floor. I let them leave my suitbag in the back of the car. Then we wait for him.

Not for long. A small oak door opens, and Gottfleisch squeezes his bulk through. He should have had the builders fit double doors. He wears a soft grey suit in a Prince of Wales check, a loud tie and a striped shirt. It looks like Yves Saint Laurent dressed the Michelin Tyre Man.

"Mickey, dear boy, welcome back. All went well?"

"I have the painting. Did Strachey ring yet?"

"Minutes ago, dear boy, from Yugoslavia." He rubs his hands together. "Well, don't keep us in suspense, Mickey. Open the case."

"Open my case?"

"Yes, yes, don't be shy."

"Why should I open my case?"

He stops looking so smug, and it cheers me up. "You *do* have the painting, Mickey?"

"Yeah."

"Then let me see it."

"It's in the car."

"In the car? Then what is this case doing here?"

"Ask them. They brought it."

It's a small victory, but it pleases me. While one of his scowlers slinks off to fetch my suitbag, Gottfleisch tells the other to make me a drink. I ask for water.

"Water?"

"Straight from the tap. I drank a lot of strange stuff over there, but I did miss a glass of Thames water."

"Extraordinary." But he sends the other hulk muttering to the kitchen. We are alone.

"How's my mother, Gottfleisch? I didn't like that phone call."

"I won't pretend that she's doing well."

"She said 'Don't let him take me away'. What were you doing to her?"

He sighs. He has the sort of face where a sigh is a lot of puff. "We tried to help her, but she's so stubborn. I have to tell you, dear boy, she suffers delusions. She imagines things. It's the drugs, of course."

"She didn't have delusions before."

Hulk Number Two reappears with my water. Gottfleisch continues talking, as if my mother's health was a matter of general interest. "I'm afraid you'll have to reconcile yourself to the fact that she is on her final descent. She is going to die, Mickey. That's why she isn't in hospital. There's no point."

I stand clutching my glass like it's a post to hold on to. Gottfleisch is my one source of information. I have to listen to him.

"The nurse helps her get some sleep, so she doesn't tire herself unavoidably. She's asleep now. She sleeps all day. She only wakes in the evening, to wait for your call. You didn't call last night."

"No."

He watches me, his head cocked to one side. You might have thought the silence was out of consideration for my feelings. If it was, it does not last long. The guy holding my suitbag asks should he open it. I step forward to do it myself.

The two bruisers crowd round me. Gottfleisch shoos them out of his light. I unzip the bag, slip my hand down to pull the tag, then tear back the inner lining.

You know how it is. There's that deathly cold moment when your fingers scrabble unseen, when the three of them hover over you, when you know the painting has disappeared. Your heart skips. A gallon of sweat bursts out like sudden dew. It lasts less than a second. Then I feel the hard paper that contains the parcel, and I slide it out.

To two of us, the painting means something. To me it means lost sleep and considerable aggravation. To Gottfleisch it means profit.

Maybe I do him an injustice. From the way he drools over it, holding it up to the light in a manner much less critical than Strachey's, maybe it means Art to him. Maybe it means History. Maybe it means he hasn't heard Strachey say that half the world's rarest Old Masters have not a scrap of the old master's own paint left on them. Maybe he just likes Raphael. Somebody must.

I will say this: when Gottfleisch excuses himself to take the Raphael out of the room, a piece of magic leaves with him. The room seems stale and flat. Something was lost. It could have been the painting. Or it could have been that the painting had become a part of me, and has been torn away.

Maybe that's what Art is.

Anyway, I sit here waiting in the dull company of two lumps of meat it means nothing to. Then Gottfleisch returns, with a cheque in his hand and a smile on his face like a satisfied snake. I take his cheque. He stands waiting. He would.

"What is this, Gottfleisch—a down payment?"

"I'm pleased with you, Mickey. It's been a good start to our relationship."

"When do I get the rest?"

"That is the agreed fee."

"Is it hell. Since when was the fee eight and a half thousand?"

"A little over that, Mickey."

"Whatever. Do you want this conversation in front of these bobos? Do you want them to hear the numbers involved?"

"Why not? You've already blurted them out. I'm sure they're jealous. Not bad for a week's work, wouldn't you say, boys?"

"We agreed half of one per cent. That's twenty-five thousand dollars."

"My dear boy—"

"Don't 'dear boy' me. We are talking twenty-five thousand dollars."

"I recall an agreed figure of ten thousand."

"Ten is not eight and half."

"There have been some expenses while you've been away."

"Expenses?"

"Medical care. Twenty-four-hour nursing doesn't come cheap."

"You said *you* would organize that."

"So I did. But you can't expect me to *pay* for it, Mickey. She's not my mother."

It is at this point I blow my top. I jump up shouting, and the two meatballs roll closer. I see now why they are still in the room. Gottfleisch begins to distance himself. "I have it fully converted and detailed," he purrs. "Nursing at six hundred dollars a week: that's the biggest element. Oncology fee, three hundred and thirty-five. Consultant on call, three hundred and ninety dollars. Drugs eighty-six. Miscellaneous travel etcetera, thirty-seven."

I am seething by this point, but he continues: "Which makes a grand total so far—because from here on the medical arrangements are up to you, Mickey—a grand total of fourteen hundred and forty-eight dollars. Excluding some odd cents. So the net due to you is eight thousand, five hundred and fifty-two dollars. As on your cheque. If you were on the payroll, of course, you might have been covered by medical insurance."

Gottfleisch is beginning to slide towards the door. It is clear that I will not slip past these two orang-utans to get at him. He continues, as if summing up at a dull board-meeting: "The fee was ten thousand American dollars, and you were happy with it. I have already paid out a million more than the asking price. I am not paying you a bonus on top."

"You'd already budgeted for that extra million."

"Did Strachey tell you that? Naughty girl. Yes, it was in the budget, but that's neither here nor there."

He is oozing out the door now, but he stops to sweet-talk me one last time. "You have eight and a half thousand dollars there, Mickey. Why not pop it into your bank account, sleep on it, see how you feel in the morning?"

"Damn you, Gottfleisch!" I kick a small coffee table across the room. "Give me my money."

"Look what you've done to that table."

He looks genuinely upset. It lies in several pieces. His body-guards lurch towards me, to show that they too can break things.

"Hold it," warns Gottfleisch, and we wait for what he has to say. "To replace that table, Mr Starr, will cost approximately twelve hundred and fifty pounds sterling. I shall expect payment within the week. I advise you not to try my gratitude any further. Go now. Go in peace."

The hospital ward smells of linoleum. Between sturdy metal beds, I walk up the central corridor, wondering what to say. By other bedsides, the few huddled visitors seem equally unsure.

Near the end of the big ward I sit down by the bed. I nod at the gladioli in the vase.

"I thought you'd have enough flowers," I say. "So I brought you these."

I drop a pile of magazines on the bedside locker. Calvin looks at me without speaking.

"I just heard about this," I say. "I should have known it was what they'd do. I'm sorry, Cal. Truly."

"Bastard," he says. His face is still swollen. He wears bandages on his arms.

"Yeah," I agree. "But I'm also sorry—for what that's worth. Tell me, after doing this, did Gottfleisch let you off the debt?"

"You must be joking, man. I still got to pay."

"How much is it now?"

He shrugs. "If I know that bastard, it will be a little bit more than I bring with me on the day I go to pay. Where I going to get that kind of money?"

"He'll think of something."

Calvin does not raise his head from the pillow. Against the starched white hospital linen his face looks grey and drained, the colour of burnt cinders. I ask, "How long will you be out of action?"

Calvin licks his lips. He doesn't want to talk to me.

"I hate Gottfleisch too," I tell him. "But I'm not with him any more."

Calvin looks like he finds this hard to believe. "He kick you out too, man, eh? That what you asking me to believe?"

"I'm getting out. There's a few things I got to do first."

He doesn't say anything. Instead of asking what it is I intend to do, he cocks an eyebrow. I am glad to see that the muscles of his face still work. I ask how long he expects to be laid up.

He thinks about it. Maybe he just thinks about whether to speak to me. He mutters, "Six weeks."

"What would you pick up normally—two hundred a week?"

He shrugs. He doesn't want this conversation. He doesn't want me here.

I say, "Six weeks at two hundred means I owe you twelve hundred pounds. Plus you are gonna find you owe Gottfleisch around eight hundred. So I'll give you two thousand. You'll get it in a week."

Calvin takes several seconds to respond. "Why you doing this?"

"I owe it you."

He sniffs. "Gottfleisch owes me compensation, not you."

"It was his money."

"I think it best not to wake her," the nurse said.

So for two hours I have waited. I was never good at waiting. This is the house I have lived in all my life, and suddenly it isn't home. The atmosphere is wrong. Maybe it comes from the nurse having been here full-time. She is more at home than I am. She pads confidently from lounge to bedroom, from bedroom to kitchen. When she uses the lavatory, it flushes with a different sound. All these years with only the two of us using it, the flush sounded homely. Now it jars. The nurse has gone three times in the last two hours.

She has her belongings in the lounge—women's magazines, her bag, a box of sweets. The radio is tuned to a different station. She has moved the chairs. I feel as if the house was up for sale, and the new owner moved in before we could move out. I don't belong here any more.

And it's too warm. She has put the central heating on—in June, for Christ's sake. The place is airless. All the air that we made here, Deptford air, our air, has been sucked out.

The house itself looks different. There are stains and scuffs on the paintwork that I never noticed before. The wallpaper needs changing. When I went in my own bedroom, it had been tidied. Things had been put away. The bed had been made with hospital corners. I came out: it wasn't my room.

I feel like I'm in a hotel. Not staying long. Just waiting.

I can see what has happened. She has turned this place into a cottage hospital. Just now, when she said I could come up and see Ma, she was making a concession. It's visiting time: don't stay too long. As I followed her up the stairs, I thought I'd have to boot out the room. But just as I turned on her, she scurried out, looking at her watch. Leave the patient with the visitor, just for a little while. It's part of the treatment.

Damn Gottfleisch. "She's gonna die, Mickey. She's on her final descent." The slob is right. I had always thought that Ma's last days would be a fading away—hollow eyes, sunken cheeks, thin skin. I was wrong. Her face has puffed up like a half-deflated balloon, and her skin is like powdered rubber. She has fever in her eyes.

Only her hands look scrawny. She clutches at the sheet with a chicken's talons. Beneath the skin, the flesh has melted away. Only bones remain. Around her papery, old lady's neck she wears a crucifix on a chain. Against that desiccated skin it shines bright and new. Her twitching fingers brush against it above the sheet, and she grasps its little gold cross. It seems to calm her. When it is safe in her hand, she lets her eyes roll upwards to gaze into the middle distance. She has the fervent piety of a figure from an old Russian icon, thinly painted on the wood.

She tries to speak, and the breath in her throat is like the sound of a turkey gobbling. The loose wrinkled skin in her neck is like a turkey's crop. Her head jerks on the pillow.

Her eyes focus on me. She stops fidgeting with the crucifix, and lets it rest between her fingers. The old smile struggles back on to her face, and the old creases return. Her eyes are bright as wet seashells. All the life in her body is concentrated there.

"Is it good to be home, son?"

"Yes," I lie. "It's great to be back."

"Did your job go well?"

"Everything's fine."

"Thank the Lord."

For a while she lies quietly, watching me. Slowly the breath drifts back into her lungs, and she gets ready to speak again.

"Don't talk if it tires you, Ma."

Her head lifts from the pillow. "I've been waiting to talk. There's so much to say now. I love to talk."

Then she waits for her lungs to refill. I sit listening to the street outside. Kids are playing football. They don't care that it's summertime. They won't play summer sports: cricket and tennis are not played around here. The only game worth playing is football. That's what they play. Always. They always have, and they always will. It is part of their life. It is part of our street.

"I was thinking," Ma says. "We should have a holiday. It would be nice to get away."

I pat her hand. "Where d'you want to go?"

Her eyes are closing. "Somewhere sunny. Somewhere warm."

I continue stroking her fragile fingers until she seems to fall asleep. Then I withdraw my hand. "Don't go," she says.

"I'm still here."

"Sometimes I have to rest from talking. It's the pain. It wells up inside me. It's difficult to . . ."

"I know, Ma, I know."

"You don't!" She almost shouts it. "No one knows. They can't."

Then, of course, she starts coughing. At first I try to soothe her, but after five seconds I jump up to run for the nurse.

Ma sleeps fitfully, dwarfed in her bed. The nurse is back in our sitting-room—knitting, or whatever it is nurses do to while away the boredom. It is her last night. I am in the kitchen, drinking tea. The phone rings.

When I open the kitchen door, the nurse is already out of the sitting-room. "I'd forgotten you were here," she says.

I pick up the receiver. It's a call from Yugoslavia. I gesture the nurse out of sight, and she goes slowly.

"Hallo Strachey. How's Belgrade?"

"Sunny but turbulent. *Perestroika* with boots on. All day long there have been demonstrations—Serbian nationalists ranting through the streets. Quite colourful, really."

The sound of her voice lifts my chin off my chest. Despite what she is saying, it is as if she is ramming sunny Belgrade air down the receiver. I smell the tang of pine trees under blue skies. Even when she asks after Ma, she babbles with happiness. She laughs when we talk of Gottfleisch.

"Don't start a vendetta, Mickey. There's no point. The main thing is that he accepted the painting."

"And stung me."

"You stung him."

"How d'you mean?"

"The painting is a fake."

I heave my mind back to how we left things. "But we made Leonid swap it back."

"Not exactly."

At first I think she is saying that Leonid cheated us once again. Then she explains. While they were alone together on the boat, she says, he admitted what we'd guessed. There was no way we could take the real Raphael out of Leningrad. There never had been. Right from the start, it was a scam.

The way it worked, of course, was like this. Lenny's contact in the Hermitage could arrange occasional *loans* of the real Raphael, to be checked out and verified by whatever experts Leonid reeled in.

"There were others, then?"

"Oh yes. Leonid sold that Raphael several times. The same technique every time."

"Didn't anyone else see through him?"

"He says not. But he would say that, wouldn't he?"

After Leonid had convinced her that never in a million years could the real painting come out, they sat on the boat working out a way everyone could stay ahead. Strachey became part of the scam. Leonid produced two of his fakes, she verified one of them, I smuggled it home.

"The only person you were fooling was me. Why didn't you tell me?"

"You still had to convince Gottfleisch."

"And you just let Leonid get away with it?"

"We had no choice. I couldn't let you go back to Gottfleisch and say we'd lost his five million."

"Leonid wouldn't have dared cash that cheque. We'd have exposed him."

"The KGB knew all about it, darling, didn't they? There was nothing to expose."

Darling. It stops me in my tracks. It actually stops me talking. She continues: "Four or five million a sale. By the time this game is finished, the KGB—or a handful of people in it—should have brought in at least twenty million dollars, all in precious hard currency."

And Gottfleisch thought Russians weren't bothered about money.

Leonid and Strachey struck a deal. Leonid could keep the authentic Raphael, and Strachey would verify the fake. As long as she convinced Gottfleisch, he in turn would convince his buyer. For the next few years, the buyer would hide his contraband anyway, so everyone would be satisfied. But Leonid could not keep the extra million-dollar uplift. That was Strachey's fee. Leonid agreed to add his signature to Gottfleisch's on the cheque, so she could draw it for cash. If he didn't sacrifice that extra mark-up, she told him, she would blow the deal apart. She had only to tell Gottfleisch, and he'd make sure the news exploded through the art market. Cancelling all future deals. Set against twenty million plus, Strachey's one million looked cheap. It was bunce to Leonid anyway. If Gottfleisch had refused to up his offer, he could have had the painting for the original four million. Fair enough for a fake.

"This million dollars, Strachey?"

"We've got it."

"You've got a million dollars in cash?"

"*We've* got a million dollars, Mickey, in a fresh account here, waiting till you arrive."

"Are you seriously including me in this, Strachey?"

"Do you seriously think I couldn't? Don't you want to share a million dollars with me, Mickey?"

What do you say to a question like that? I take a gulp of air and ask how long she is staying out there in the sun.

"I move tomorrow. But only to Dubrovnik. Do you know it? It's a beautiful old fortress city, perched above the blue Adriatic. Do I sound like a brochure?"

"Better."

"When are you coming?"

I can't answer that right now. I tell her to ring again tomorrow evening with her Dubrovnik phone number. I say she had better clear the line now, because this call must be costing her a fortune. She laughs. "We can afford it, darling."

She hangs up.

She is the only one who had her head screwed on. From the moment she sniffed the air last Wednesday, she saw things straight. Gottfleisch didn't see straight: he thought he was rich enough to buy anything, even a national treasure. Leonid didn't see straight: he thought he could fool her. And until she rang, I didn't see straight: I thought I had to get back at Gottfleisch. I should have known better. I've tried burning things down before. If I got Gottfleisch, his men would get me. If they didn't, the law would do it for them.

I guess I should take a leaf out of Strachey's book: compromise. It may not make me feel like a super-hero, but at least I can live happy.

Like I say, Strachey knows best. And she calls me darling.

There are some summer days when blue skies disappear in a short gust of wind. This is one of those days. Clouds race across the sky at a hundred miles an hour. One minute the sun is out. The next it's hidden. Then it is out again. Suddenly, rain falls sharp and warm. Clouds roll away. The whole sky is blue.

Those warm splinters of rain dash against Ma's bedroom window. From the hollow she has seared in the banked pillows, she struggles to raise her head. I lower my head closer to her dry lips.

"I need to talk to you," she says. "You've got to help me."

Here she grabs my arm with surprising strength. "There's been enough pain. I don't want any more. I can't go on living like this."

Gently, I remove her wrinkled hand from my arm, and press it between my warm palms. "I understand, Ma," I say. "Trust me. Everything will turn out fine."

As the clock approaches midnight, I sit in the fireside chair beside her. She lies on her side watching me, and as the minutes tick away we gaze into each other's faces. The house is silent. I wait for her to fall asleep, but she can't. Maybe she's had too much sleep already. Maybe she's excited.

I guess that's it. While I sit here in the chair, she is unable to drift off. My eyes are the ones that close. I've been so tired. Suddenly, I fall asleep, leaving her lying there watching me, thinking a mother's thoughts, wondering how her son feels.

She may have watched me for an hour. I don't know. Eventually she will have drifted unwillingly to sleep.

When I awake much later, my back has stiffened into the shape of this upright chair. I stand up slowly. The springs of the seat groan as my weight leaves them. When I move, my joints creak. It is almost five o'clock.

Round the edges of the curtain creeps a grey half-light. Somewhere out there, a blackbird sings. Other birds join in.

The room is so still now that when I take a pace forward I have to brush the air aside. The sound of my breathing is like waves on a distant beach. But to hear my mother's faint sighs I have to lean close above her face. Inside her troubled dream she detects my presence, and she frowns.

When I lift her head an inch from her bank of pillows, she does not wake. She is sleeping soundly. The drugs have numbed her. She has fallen through the sleep into the unconsciousness that is her normal state.

I slide the topmost pillow out, and lower her head back on to the next. With her pillow cradled warm and soft in my arms, I bend down. I kiss her on the forehead. Then I kiss her eyes. Then I lay the pillow gently across her face, and press the edges in against her cheeks.

There is no struggle. She does stir beneath my pressure, a few tiny convulsions as her nervous system involuntarily fights the suffocation. But I press firmly on the downy pillow. I have to do it. I am her son. I cannot let her life drag through this painful conclusion. It has to end. Even now is too late. She wants me to remember who she really was, not this seeping husk, decaying between white sheets. She has nothing to live for now, except more pain and humiliation. I can spare her those. Because I love her, I will take her life. As gently as I can.

Soon she lies still. So there will be no chance she might revive, I leave the pillow pressed against her face for another full minute. Sixty long seconds. Then I lift it away, and look at what I've done.

In death she is light and fragile, as insubstantial as moonlight in shallow water. Her face is etched with immovable pain-lines, and she has died with a frown creasing her brow. I try to smooth it away, but the flesh is unresponsive.

I replace the pillow beneath her head. I tidy her hair. I smooth the sheet. They will say that she died peacefully in her sleep.

I walk across to the window, and open the curtain. When I look down into the familiar street, it means nothing. In my stockinged feet, I creep back across the room. It is as if I am afraid I might waken her.

At the door, I turn to look for one last time.

In her cold, neatly made bed she lies tiny and still. She is at peace. It is over. Gradually, the room will fill with daylight.